AN ALIEN BY CIRCUMSTANCE

DAVID BARNETT

MINERVA PRESS
MONTREUX LONDON WASHINGTON

AN ALIEN BY CIRCUMSTANCE
Copyright © David Barnett 1996

All Rights Reserved

No part of this book may be reproduced in any form,
by photocopying or by any electronic or mechanical means,
including information storage or retrieval systems,
without permission in writing from both the copyright owner
and the publisher of this book.

ISBN 1 85863 962 X

First Published 1996 by
MINERVA PRESS
195 Knightsbridge
London SW7 1RE

Printed in Great Britain by
B.W.D. Ltd., Northolt, Middlesex

AN ALIEN BY CIRCUMSTANCE

Love is so many things:

        Respect

        Understanding

        Acceptance

        Touching

        Trust

        Forgiveness

        Gentleness

        Strength

        So many things...

ACKNOWLEDGEMENTS

I've been blessed to have had loving parents, Easton and Madge Barnett. I'm blessed to have my brothers, Paul and Michael, whom I love very much.

I would like to thank Denise for being a life-time friend; Norman and Elaine for caring; and Jules for the feedback. Thanks also go out to all my friends and associates, past and present, who have helped in some way to shape this book.

Last, but not least, I would like to thank you, the reader, for making the choice to read my work. I certainly hope that you will enjoy it.

Love is our guide in life and so I leave you now to read on with love in my heart.

PART I

1

Dwayne was in seventh heaven as he lay on the sun-drenched sands of Hellshire beach, baking slowly. It had been several years since he had last visited Jamaica and so he intended to make the most of his stay, soaking up every iota of sun, sea and sand. As he sifted the soft white sand between his fingers he began to fantasise about the tall, dark beauty who had entered the sea moments ago. A woman of confidence, wearing a rather skimpy bikini over her tight hourglass figure.

Suddenly remembering where he was, Dwayne turned his attention to the smell of bami and fried fish wafting from the small huts nearby.

"Fancy some fish?" he called to the rest of his family, who were busy splashing around in the clear blue waters that attracted so many people to this small enclave of paradise.

"Good idea!" his mum shouted back, with his sister, Quisha, and his brother, Wesley, beaming in agreement. Dwayne was the youngest of the three, being ten months younger than Quisha and near to three years younger than Wesley. In his youth this gap had seemed enormous. Now in his late twenties, the gap had dwindled to insignificance with all three sharing a common stage in their lives. The one where you're pushing thirty and wondering where the time's gone.

Dwayne smiled to himself as his teeth dug into the crispy coating around the bami. He hadn't felt this content for a long while. Since his father had died over two years back he hadn't really felt able to let himself go, to have fun. Biting into the fish now and savouring every morsel was wonderful.

"Mmmm ... this is good," oozed Quisha.

"I'll second that!" smirked Wesley.

"Eh buoy, pu dong de fish befor mi slap yu ina ya ed back!" came the cook's voice in the background.

They all laughed – there was always some drama going on between the locals. In fact, Dwayne couldn't imagine J.A. without the drama. Whether in the marketplace, the bus, or the patti shop; one could always rely on some irate individual cursing their neighbour. Dwayne mused over whether this was just down to lifestyle or too much sun. He couldn't make up his mind which so he spurted out,

"Wa ya tink guys, a de heat or a de lifestyle, why Jamaicans so excitable?" Dwayne liked to feel that he was versatile in terms of speaking the Jamaican patoi.

"Bwoy a de heat, mann," quipped Wesley in response. If he had locks they would have splayed across his face as he now tossed his head back, shaking it from side to side. He grinned over at his brother who was revelling in his comical attempt at being rootsy. Deep inside, all of them were aware of a cultural yearning that had gone unheeded for a long time. Quisha joined in.

"Cha dem jus na av nuff hec-citement a home."

"What do you reckon, Mum?" asked Dwayne, turning his head to face her. Hyacinth smiled.

"Mi na nor ... " she said lackadaisically, then took another bite of her fried snapper.

Having had the thought for the day, everyone continued with the meal in silence. Heading back to the sea for a final dip, Dwayne spotted the girl that he admired earlier heading his way. He stuck his chest out instinctively, then proceeded to stride in a more determined manner toward the water. I wonder if she'll notice me – maybe it's my lucky day, thought Dwayne to himself. The demi-goddess glanced at Dwayne briefly, then walked by with indifference. "Maybe not," said Dwayne quietly to himself.

They were doing the rounds and the day had come for them to visit Aunt Sybil. She was a large, well-built, well-meaning woman, but Dwayne always felt a little apprehensive about seeing her.

"It'll be another third degree," said Dwayne quietly to Quisha, as they pulled up outside the house.

"Tell me about it," said Quisha in a matter of fact way. Everyone stepped out of the taxi, stretching their legs as they did so. Hyacinth knocked the gate with a small stone that had been lying on the rough sidewalk moments before. Moments later, out came Sybil in a tropical print dress; she was beaming with excitement.

"Lard de hinglish people dem finally harrive sah."

Sybil then proceeded to hug everyone in her gentle way. Once settled on the veranda, she offered them all some cool lemonade which was gratefully received. The heat was oppressive today with no breeze to keep the air moving. Dwayne gulped down his glass of lemonade thankfully and impatiently. "So how de girlfriend dem?" enquired Sybil as an opener.

Wesley and Dwayne looked at each other, wondering who should go first. Aunt Sybil had a way of making them feel somehow inadequate for not having girlfriends. It was not so much the probing questions but the way in which she asked; the almost accusatory tone of voice. Dwayne offered his reply first. Wesley smirked.

"Well, you know how it is Aunt, no-one serious on the horizon yet."

"Same here," chipped in Wesley hurriedly, but trying to sound noncommittal at the same time. This vague, almost non-response from the two males forced Sybil to turn her attention to the one eligible female in the family.

"And you, Quisha henny, nice young man fi tell mi bout." She reached forward to pat Quisha's knee.

"Mmmm ... well, I'm seeing a guy called James right now; he's kind of cute you know." She didn't bother to mention that he was a white guy. This she knew would have gone down like a lead balloon with her aunt and was already a source of contention with her mother. Hyacinth wasn't a racist, but she had endured much prejudice in her time from various quarters. Her attitude now was that life was made much simpler by sticking to one's own colour.

Dwayne smiled to himself at this point, he had often thought of asking his friend Lisa out. He still wanted to feel her tongue sliding passed his as their lips pressed against each other. He could visualise her bright green eyes blazing with a radiance that was joy itself. Her petite nose and kissable red lips. He imagined now running his hand up to the small of her back in order to press her closely to him. Lisa was now saying to him,

"You're my teddy bear." Dwayne pulled his face back from hers, his wide dark lips puckered.

"What do ya mean, you're not trying to say I'm soft are you?"

"Yes you are ... and you're cuddly," she said cupping his face in her hands and squeezing gently. She then pushed her thin bony nose up against his equally bony nose bridge. His wider nostrils flared as she stared into his watery eyes.

"You're tickling me," he could hear himself saying as she gently rubbed her hands up and down his rib cage.

Sybil interrupted Dwayne's thoughts in a manner that caused him to jerk his head up sharply. "Buoy Dwayne look more like im fader each day."

"Ihh," said Hyacinth lazily in agreement. Dwayne was light skinned like his father had been, but much taller and slimmer. His features were strong but sensitive, a quality he seemed drawn to in others.

"I don't kow about that," interrupted Quisha, "I think Wesley looks more like Dad. He's got Dad's build and eyes." Being of a more solid build than Dwayne, Wesley was smiling with self-adulation and anyway it felt good to be likened to one's dad. It was reassuring at least, especially coming from a culture where having a different father for each child wasn't uncommon. Quisha didn't actually seem to resemble either of her parents, not in an obvious way at any rate. She was much darker than both of them and had the long wavy hair of her grandmother. It was her full cherry-coloured lips and pretty smile that gave her away as Hyacinth's daughter. The afternoon dragged on lazily with everyone making relaxed, congenial conversation.

2

Dwayne felt every nerve in his body tingling as the cool spray from the shower invigorated a body that was still waking up. God this is good, he thought to himself, I feel like I'm alive ... really alive. It was a bright sunny morning and Dwayne felt ready for anything. As he left the bath, he dried off briskly whilst whistling to himself. He then pulled on a pair of briefs before getting down to his daily routine of press-ups. "Should I do a few more?" he thought out loud (thirty was his usual limit). "Naa." With a twinge in his right bicep this seemed a wise decision.

With only two days left of the family holiday, Dwayne wanted to make the most of today. He didn't know what he would be doing when he got back to England, or where he would be living. He had rashly given up his job as an office administrator with a law firm in London. The holiday had seemed like the perfect opportunity to chuck in a job which was boring him to death and to get a fresh perspective on life. It seemed like only yesterday when he was pinching himself in a toilet cubicle in order to wake himself up. The toilet had become a place of refuge from the daily grind of the office. Dwayne knew that he had to get out of the trench that he'd dug himself into. Life was dull with a capital D and this was draining all the energy from him.

"Does any one want to come shopping?" came Wesley's question to the family.

"Yeh!" was the resounding response. A taxi was ordered and they all piled in. No-one felt like roughing it on a packed minibus today. Dwayne, and his mum in particular, found the ignorant behaviour that went on trying to board one of these vehicles rather trying. The pushing, shoving and bad manners really grated on their sensibilities. As the taxi sped along Old Hope Road, Dwayne took in the warmth of the breeze against his skin. The car horns and loud exhausts faded away as Dwayne went back in his mind to when Kingston had been a happy and relaxed place.

"Hurry up, Wesley and Dwayne, or you'll be late for school," had chirped his mother up the stairs of their comfortable town house.

"Buoy dem pitney deh av it easy dem day ya," chirped in his father light-heartedly as Dwayne raced down stairs ahead of Wesley.

Five minutes later Wesley ambled down at his usual pace. "Wesley you're too laid back for your own good," chided his father.

"When me and your mum was growing up we couldn't afford to be late, yah noah – or else is serious trouble – huh (he grunted at this point for dramatic effect) Na tru Hyacinth?"

"Uh-hu," she chipped in. Dwayne smiled over his cornmeal porridge. Every morning was the same speech. Quisha, as usual, was well organised and had by now eaten her porridge; helped their mum prepare sandwiches for their lunch break; and had settled into her usual chair at the table with a copy of the comic *Gleaner*. Five minutes later they filed passed their mum to receive the usual peck on the cheek and similarly filed passed their dad, but this time to collect their daily pocket money. The sun was beginning to get hot out on Hope Road as they all filed on to the large green J.O.S. bus heading up town. Everyone seemed to be calm and polite as they said their good mornings to familiar faces.

"Step up for me, baby," said the conductress in a motherly tone to Quisha as her brothers protectively brought up the rear.

Now it was just dog eat dog. Still, maybe London wasn't so different, Dwayne mused. Just that people were steeped in the tradition of queuing though resenting your very presence. After much discussion with his siblings, he had come to the conclusion that it was the political and economic climate that was responsible for the hostile spirit within the island. Maybe that was what was responsible for the damp spirit back home. Dwayne felt that things would change – they had to, Dwayne was an optimist.

Twingate Plaza was bustling with the midday shoppers, mainly from the middle classes of uptown and the enclaves of tourist city. Lisa Stanfield's 'Poison' was emanating from a nearby boutique that Dwayne was entering. The others had gone to seek out their own tastes and they had arranged to meet again at a prearranged rendezvous time of two o'clock. Dwayne scanned the racks hungrily. He mused over a baggy pair of black trousers but then left them where they were. Poor imitations of style were not for Dwayne. The T-shirt rack offered him something more exciting. Moments later he left the store with two brightly coloured T-shirts neatly folded in the Second Avenue bag. He smiled to himself, the Jamaica Irie T-shirt would be for his best friend, Pete, back in Cambridge. His next port of call was to be Photo Quick to pick up the last of the holiday snaps.

He always felt a little bit anxious when opening up a pouch of goodies. Having attained some recognition as a photographer he felt that his professional status was always being put to the test, whether formally or informally. It was the photography that had kept him sane during his two years at the law firm. It was a therapeutic distraction from the mundane job that he saw as an endurance test, a cross to bear. His art had given him purpose in what had become a banal existence. His recent exhibition in a small gallery on the fringes of London's West End gave him the satisfaction of being recognised in an art world full of pretension and bullshit. Dwayne wanted to cut through all that. Dwayne smiled as he pulled the snaps out of their envelope.

"No heads cut off so far," he said in a friendly manner to the young woman sitting next to him. He felt in a chatty mood and this girl looked receptive. She smiled back to him in response. It was just then that Dwayne registered how attractive she was. Her sensuous lips curled upward, her tight hazelnut skin stretched over her high cheek bones, and her large brown eyes smiled back at him. Those eyes could have melted him to the spot. Typical, he thought to himself – why do I always meet someone I fancy under the most unconducive of circumstances. He didn't pursue further conversation at this juncture, but got up suddenly and headed for the door. Instinct had cut in there – it was a matter of self-preservation. He knew that this girl was interested but experience had taught him that holiday flings were not for him – his heart always misread the rules.

Four years ago he had his first sexual experience with a Canadian black girl called Jackie. Like Dwayne she was holidaying with her family in Montego Bay and they had met at the reggae festival called Sunsplash. Her dark skin complemented her long black plaited hair. The silver and gold beads which hung on the ends of each fine strand, framed her dimpled cheeks. Her pointed chin and sultry lips seemed to move in unison whenever she smiled, which was frequently. That was what had really attracted him to Jackie in the first place. Her dark mysterious eyes were a bonus. After dating for only three nights he had sex with her down on the beach, during the early hours of the morning. Paradoxically, it was the only place they could find with any privacy, away from the prying eyes of the family.

"What now?" Dwayne had asked in a voice all breathless with the raptures of orgasm. "What now?"

Silence greeted this question as Jackie's eyelids closed against his gaze. What was there to say – they had their fun and tomorrow was a new day. Numb silence hung in the air as they lay together quietly naked until the crickets stopped their singing and the sun began to rise. Dwayne sighed heavily as his mind wandered back to the present.

He marched on quickly toward the record store over the road. Twenty more minutes to browse before getting back to the others. Dwayne tossed this around in his mind for a few seconds, then changed course for the souvenir shop.

Cha, they probably haven't got what I want in there anyway. The repetitive dance hall sounds escaping from what was aptly called the Record Shack were not indicative of a haven for a funkster like Dwayne.

Once in the souvenir shop Dwayne studied and marvelled at the works of art alongside the trinkets and plastic sundries. He loved the carvings and sculptures reminiscent of his African heritage, and the metallic looking pots with South American overtones. Jamaica was indeed a melting pot of many cultures and races.

Realising the time he quickly picked out a few postcards from the rack by the cash register, paid for them and was just about to walk out when the oriental lady behind the cash register called after him.

"Eh, you is hinglish man don't it – mi recognise de haccent, buoy it nice you nuh. Dash some more lyrics mec we ear nuh."

Dwayne was amused by the ladies fascination with his accent and had become quite used to this kind of request. How ironic, thought Dwayne. In Jamaica I'm seen as an English man and in England a West Indian – belonging to both places and yet to neither. Dwayne quickly gathered his wits, aware now of the other eyes that were settling on him from other quarters in the shop; he smiled sheepishly.

"Sorry," he said whilst pulling on the shop door. In his haste to leave he forgot about the step outside and nearly went headlong into a rather harassed-looking lady, laden with shopping. "Sorry," he said again.

Back at the rendezvous point, Mamas Patties, everyone looked contented with their morning's venture. Dwayne sat down next to his mum.

"Everything okay, people?"

"Yep," came the resounding reply.

"Well then, let's attack some of these great smelling patties," smirked Dwayne.

3

Friday had come – Quisha pouted.
"Crumbs, this holiday went too fast, man, I was only just unwinding," said Wesley.
"Same here," echoed Dwayne. "Still, I'm glad that we're visiting Uncle Charlie today, so we go on a high."
Charlie knew how to have a good time and always made them laugh. The mean undertones pervading the island's people had left Charlie untouched. The family embraced Charlie as he welcomed them through the wrought iron gates in front of the house. Charlie's broad frame moved gracefully toward the front porch while the sun bounced off the back of his bald shiny head.
"Buoy, it nice and cool pan de veranda sah," cooed Hyacinth as she nestled into a white wicker armchair.
"Yeh man," confirmed Wesley as he glided into a chair next to his mother. Dwayne and Quisha, looking somewhat laboured in their steps, dropped into some matching armchairs opposite Wesley and Hyacinth. Charlie hurried off for some much needed refreshments.
The chink-chink of cool ice in a glass jug was like music to Dwayne's ears. The heat seemed particularly oppressive today – Dwayne could feel a damp sticky patch growing under his armpits. He pulled his arms in towards his body in a guarded fashion as he was always fearful of smelling in the company of other people.
"So, where is Ida then?" enquired Hyacinth after a few sips of the cool lemonade, her lipstick smeared on the glass. Ida was Charlie's wife, a rather quiet sombre woman which seemed a direct personality clash with Charlie's gregarious character; a source of much debate amongst the family.
"Buoy, look like her mudder na well ya know, Hyacinth. So she gan a country fi go visit er."
"Nothing too serious is it?" Hyacinth's tone was now showing more concern and she had dropped the patoi accent.
"Mi na know broder, mi check seh she aving some blood pressure problem." He kissed his teeth with frustration. "After she won res er self. She jus up an dung. A woman of eighty-tree, I ask yu." Charlie then changed his tone, becoming more up-beat. "So mi eer seh de wedder in hingland a himprove."

"No easy drought wedder dem a talk bout brodder," cut in Hyacinth.

"Can we watch your satellite for a bit, Uncle?" asked Wesley, realising the familiar ground that the conversation was now following.

"Yes man," quipped Charlie in his matter of fact manner. Habitually Wesley, Quisha and Dwayne removed their sandals before stepping on to the deep pile of the lounge carpet. The afternoon ran on in a leisurely fashion for everyone. With Hyacinth's offspring dipping into the conversation between her and Charlie intermittently, between copious amounts of MTV.

Dwayne felt a queasiness in his stomach and a sadness in his heart when it came time to leave. Snatching time here and there with a loved one was not something one got used to but simply accepted. Charlie embraced Dwayne last, patting him on the back with a heavy hand and grinning broadly. Dwayne grinned back, feeling his spirits lift. The sun shone brightly off his uncle's caramel complexion and warm features.

"Bye then – una av a safe flight and look after una selves ya eeh." Charlie waved.

4

"Dem taxi driver, dem tief!" exclaimed Hyacinth as the family entered the cool air-conditioned lounge of the airport, heading directly for the check-in desk. They all laughed. Getting ripped off for looking like tourists was a common experience for them. Hyacinth prided herself on letting the deluded individual concerned know of their bumbling stupidity by going into her life story on dual nationality. By the end of this lecture, she usually got away with a few dollars below the going rate and a good boot-licking. Everyone looked smart this morning though rather tired, as was to be expected at five o'clock in the morning. Hyacinth had on a very smart navy blue trouser suit with a low-cut neckline. Her gold loop earrings matched the gold clip on her handbag. People were often complementing her on her taste in clothes and youthful appearance. Quisha sauntered up to the desk swinging her hips to and fro as her fitted skirt and jacket clung to her. The pastel pink jacket contrasted nicely with the black skirt and blended in with her choice of lipstick. Her jet black hair blew away from her face with each step.

"Would you like to take this case from me now, Quisha?" enquired Wesley, who by this point was struggling with every step he made.

"That's okay," quipped Quisha. "You're doing a great job already." A smirk appeared on her lips, but Wesley was not amused.

"Typical," he said quietly under his breath. "So much for women's lib." His crisp white shirt was now becoming a nuisance around his neck. Dwayne was straining behind Wesley with another tan leather case.

"Out the way – out the way." He heaved it on to the scales beside the desk, then straightened his paisley tie around the stiff white collar of his shirt. "Can't wait to get on the plane," said Dwayne to himself. "I hate all this blooming palaver."

"Who's got the tickets!" snapped Wesley. Nerves were bound to be taut at this hour of the day, it seemed to go without saying, so Dwayne snapped back,

"Why are you looking at me?"

"Because you said that you were taking them," retorted Wesley as his voice level rose.

"Oh piss off," hissed Dwayne, who had lost his rag.

"Dwayne!" his mum chided, "there is no need for that language. Anyway, I have the tickets."

"Ladies and gentlemen we have now arrived at London Heathrow, please remain in your seats until the seat belt sign is switched off ..." The voice over the speaker was welcomed by applause. It was always a relief to know that you had arrived at your destination in one piece. With the occasional interruption of meal times and loud snoring from Quisha, the journey had given Dwayne the opportunity for real thought; time to reflect on his past, to think about his future. His thoughts drifted, just for a moment, to when they were up in the air.

"What do you want to do when you leave school, Dwayne? You're not even sure are you? You're just becoming a drifter. What on earth are you going to do with an art degree? Come on tell me ... tell me!" It seemed like only yesterday when his dad was badgering him.

Four years later and I still haven't used my degree, thought Dwayne wearily. What do I really want to do? What job is going to excite me, for crying out loud? Quisha's a journalist, maybe ... hmmm, I'm not much of a writer. Wesley's enjoying his job as a researcher for the BBC ... teaching ... teaching? Why on earth did that come into my head? Dwayne thought hard, furrowing his forehead. Aunt Sybil used to say how much she had enjoyed teaching when she was working. She often complained how much she missed it. I'm pretty good with kids or at least I used to be when helping Jenny out at the crèche. Jenny was an old acquaintance from Dwayne's college days. He hadn't thought about Jenny for a long while. Damn it. If I could only make some decent money out of my photography I could stick with that. Dwayne sighed, all this thinking was making him tense. He caught the attention of one of the hostesses with a 'have a nice day'-type grin fixed on her face.

"Excuse me, could I have a rum and coke please?"

"One moment, sir," came the reply as she spun around to move back down the isle.

The cool drink came as a welcome respite from his thoughts. He leant back in his seat and gazed out of the little square window next to him, not registering anything – just staring. Moments later Dwayne sank back into deep thought, oblivious to the in-flight movie which had just come on. It would be nice to give something back to education after years of taking ... to at least do something meaningful. A wave of relief passed through Dwayne, his instincts told him that this decision was the right decision. He finished his drink with a smile of contentment spreading over his face.

Here he was now stepping of the Boeing 707 knowing that a new chapter in his life was about to begin.

PART II

5

"Wow!" exclaimed Pete, his fingers gripped the T-shirt Dwayne had brought back for him. His slightly rounded features and light brown eyes were now alight. "I love it Dwayne, thanks mate. I'll try it on now." For early June Pete had a surprisingly deep tan, which showed against the thin strip of cream-coloured skin where his watch had been. Dwayne noticed this as Pete proceeded to haul off his black Levi's T-shirt.

"Have you been working out?" smirked Dwayne.

"Well, just a little," grinned Pete. "Got to keep the old bod in shape when you get to this age." They both creased up laughing. "What about you then Dwayne, been working out on some sun-drenched beach in Jamaica, honing those little biceps?" enquired Pete in a teasing manner.

"Don't push it," cut in Dwayne. "You're just jealous."

"Oh yes, let's have a look then."

Dwayne took up the challenge and slipped off the loose wine-striped shirt that he was wearing; allowing a tight torso to emerge. He grinned back at Pete as he tensed his pecs.

"Hmmm ... not bad, let's feel your biceps then."

Dwayne obligingly tensed these.

"Pretty hard."

Pete seemed to be almost flirting with Dwayne as he took on this new role as admirer. His hand rested on Dwayne's right bicep, gripping firmly but lingering there much longer than necessary. Pete's hand then moved to his right pectoral. Since confiding in his friend, Pete, about his bisexual nature, their friendship seemed to take on a new set of meanings, more complex than before. Neither party was really sure of what these meanings added up to, but enjoyed their erotic undertones nonetheless. Dwayne moved back from Pete having taken this particular game far enough.

"Did you say something about testing out some of your cooking on me?"

Pete smiled back. "The best stir-fry this side of town."

The kitchen was Pete's favourite room in his small one-bedroom flat. Being a qualified chef and working for one of the most prestigious hotels in Cambridge, Pete prided himself on his cooking.

"So what's been happening since I've been away?" enquired Dwayne.

"Well, brace yourself," said Pete in a rather droll tone. "I've met a girl and we're going steady, as they say."

Dwayne tried to conceal his surprise, with little success. "Jees ... you're finally hitched. Well ... ah ... good for you." He slapped his friend on the back in the usual man to man fashion, the only fashion deemed safe or acceptable by society. "So tell me, what's she like?"

Pete wiped a spray of saliva from his nose. "Spray it again Sam," chuckled Pete.

"Oops, sorry," replied Dwayne, only just realising the fact he was spitting. So in a calmer fashion he said, "Come on man, fill me in."

After several hours of chatter, Dwayne finally left his friend's flat, heading back across town to his mother's house.

"Hi, Mum," chirped Dwayne.

"So you decided to come home tonight?" returned Hyacinth dryly. "By the time twelve thirty came I thought you would be staying at Pete's," she continued, eyes glaring. At this point in time his mother was convinced that her son was having some sort of love affair with his friend. Since January, when Dwayne had declared his sexuality to her and the rest of the family, she had seen Pete in a different light.

Fed up with months of innuendo and sourness, Dwayne said with equal dryness, "Well you were wrong." With that he marched upstairs to his room and slammed the door. He slumped on to the bed, curling up into a ball, his hands gripping his shoulders tightly. This form of self-love was unconditional; uncomplicated; simply comforting. Dwayne let out a long, heavy sigh.

"Damn, damn," he cursed himself softly. "What a fuck up." He cursed the situation he now found himself in. He knew that family life was no longer working. He felt like cursing his mother but didn't. He thought he had done the right thing by opening up to his family, after all if he couldn't be open with them then who could he be open with. They were supposed to be there for him as he was there for them, at least that was what he had once thought. He didn't want to go back to a time of feeling weak and afraid – afraid to be himself. Thoughts of the night he opened his heart to his family flooded back to him. There had been a discussion on the television about AIDS and it's prevalence among the gay community in San Francisco. He remembered his mother's words clearly.

"Goodness me, what those people do is unnatural."

"What do you mean?" he had snapped back. "What is unnatural about one human being expressing affection for another, male or female? We all need it, you know."

"But they're so promiscuous," said Hyacinth in a holier than thou tone of voice.

"I don't believe this crap – not all homosexuals are promiscuous, just as not all heterosexuals are promiscuous." Dwayne was beginning to get really angry. "Anyway what has that got to do with anything?" The outbreak of AIDS had become a focus for all the bigotry under the sun; newspapers were calling it the gay plague or trying to determine whether or not black Africans were the real source of the disease. Hyacinth's bigoted attack was now a personal attack on her son. Every word left Dwayne reeling. He started to raise his voice well above the volume of the television. "Well, I'm bisexual so what does that make me ... eh!?" Dwayne hadn't expected his feelings to come out under these circumstances but he knew they had to come out. He was waiting for his mother to climb down from her position of judgement, to say that she had been wrong to say those things. To say that she loved him.

"I don't be-lieve it," hissed Hyacinth, "No son of mine could be ... be bisexual. No way."

"Well you had better believe it!" yelled Dwayne, as tears welled up into his eyes – feelings of rejection were hard to hide.

Quisha, trying to be helpful, got up out of her seat and said, "Come on, calm down everyone," flapping her hands whilst talking as if quelling a mob. Wesley simply sat scratching his head, saying nothing. Dwayne was brought back to the present by a light tapping on his bedroom door.

"Who is it?" he called.

"Quisha. Can I come in?"

"Yeah, sure." Dwayne pulled himself up into a sitting position on the edge of his bed. He was glad it was Quisha, she was the only one who treated him as she always had, without any of the reservation or the sarcasm that he now got from his mother and brother. He quietly hoped that one day soon the gulf would be bridged and that they would be a tight family for real.

"So how's it going?" enquired Quisha in a mild manner.
"Okay, I guess," said Dwayne half-heartedly.
"How's Pete doing then?"
"Pretty good, he's got himself a new girlfriend now, so he's on a high."
"Right on," smiled Quisha.
"Talking of which, how's it going with you and James, did you see him today?"
She flushed a little as she answered. "Well yes, I saw him today..."
"Must be going good," cut in Dwayne, picking up on her body language. "Hope you guys are being careful," he smiled at her whilst twitching his eyebrows in quick succession.
"Don't you worry little brother," said Quisha in a patronising tone of voice, having regained her composure. "So how are the PGCE applications going, got any off yet?"
Dwayne was used to Quisha changing the direction of the conversation when ever the word sex was likely to come up.
"Oh, pretty good so far – I'm fed up with the tedious forms though. I've got one more to send off to Kingston Poly and they seem to want everything but my inside leg measurement."
"Right," chuckled Quisha, "it's probably all part of the vetting procedure – to see if you've got the endurance to be a teacher."
"Must be," retorted Dwayne. "Anyway, Goldsmith's is my number one choice, there should be a real mixed crowd there."
"So you're sticking with London then?" Quisha patted Dwayne gently on the thigh whilst making this observation.
"Yep, you know me, looking for life in the fast lane. Anyway, (Dwayne's voice took on a more serious tone) at least it's cosmopolitan. I mean let's face it, half this street treats us like Martians from outer space; whilst the other half like idiots ... with their plastic smiles and surface liberalism."
Quisha sighed in acknowledgement. She knew what Dwayne meant – she shared his experience, they all had. She knew how it felt when a neighbour crossed the road as she approached, as if suddenly a land mine loomed before them. She knew how it felt when a neighbour walked by her, gazing at some imaginary object so as not to meet her gaze. Yes, she knew what he meant.

"I mean Christ, the Smedleys over the road are the only genuine neighbours that we have," blurted out Dwayne after a pause.

"I know ... I know," replied Quisha quietly.

It was eleven thirty in the morning, when Dwayne finally got out of bed. Fifteen minutes before *House on the Prairie*, he thought to himself. Still feeling half-dazed he dragged himself under the shower and turned on the faucet allowing the warm water to revive him.

Although it was still summer Dwayne was not feeling hot enough to risk a cold shower.

"Morning," he said chirpily to his mother as he entered the kitchen in a pair of washed-out jeans and a Wranglers waistcoat.

"Morning," replied Hyacinth without much enthusiasm, still sour from the night before.

So much for making an effort, thought Dwayne quietly to himself. He hated atmospheres but he was only prepared to meet his mother halfway. Being familiar with this pattern of behaviour from his mother, Dwayne knew that further conversation with her was a waste of time. Monosyllabic responses were all he would get for the time being. He reached for a cereal bowl from the rack by the sink and poured himself some muesli; then drifted into the living room to find Wesley and Quisha already tuned into Channel Four.

"Just in time for House on the Prairie," chuckled Wesley.

Quisha acknowledged her younger brother with a smile.

"Sundays just wouldn't be the same without it," came Dwayne's reply, as he dropped himself into a large cream armchair by the television. Hyacinth popped into the living room intermittently to view the show, whilst busying herself with household chores. When the credits finally came up Quisha dabbed her eyes with a tissue, whilst the two brothers forced back their tears as best they could with the blinking of eyelids and biting of lips. Still trying to regain his composure, Dwayne's voice quivered slightly as he asked his sister to pass him the *TV Weekly*.

"Nothing much on now," commented Quisha as she threw the magazine over to her brother.

"Hmmm ..." sighed Wesley as he left for his room.

"Come on, let's get dinner on the go," suggested Quisha as she got up to go to the kitchen.

"Isn't it Wesley's turn to cook?" queried Dwayne.

"Probably, but you know Wesley, he's married to his work, he won't come out of his room until he smells grub. He's never been what you could call domestic anyway." Quisha rolled her eyes as she spoke the words.

"Bloody lazy more like it," retorted Dwayne.

"That's the truth," his sister laughed – washing his eyes with saliva as she did so.

After the traditional rice and peas with fried chicken, the family lounged in front of the television, fixed to their seats. Suddenly Wesley got up and turned to face Dwayne.

"Hey, can you come to help me out for a minute?" came his request.

"Sure," said Dwayne, slightly bemused. He followed his brother into his room where papers were strewn all around. Wesley sat at his desk covered with more paper, with the addition of cups and mugs filled with stale coffee.

"I'm doing some research for a new social affairs show the Beeb's screening in November. One programme's going to be looking at why black people in this country still under-achieve within the British education system. Seeing as you've actually reached a decision to contribute to this system through which you've ... well we've all succeeded, I thought you might like to help me out here, bro, with some opinions." Bro, it had been a long time since Wesley had used this term of endearment. Dwayne sensed that the cold front between them had shifted, if only a little. He grinned at his brother, then sat down on the bed.

"Well, it's a tricky subject."

"Do you think it's to do with a lack of role models?" offered Wesley.

"To a de-gree ..." trailed Dwayne, "but think about it, we never had any more role models to follow than the next person. If anything, less ... growing up in a place like Cambridge. We had encouragement from our parents – I think that's probably the key. When I think about it though that's probably the key for all kids."

Wesley leaned forward, "So we've got the big one, parental attitude ... ri-ght?"

"Right," echoed Dwayne. There was a pause. "And I mean there's this thing about selling out and taking on white aspirations isn't there?"

"Hmm ... in some circles," admitted Wesley. "But maybe that's more to do with a system that has discriminated and continues to discriminate against black people. You know what I mean – Euro centric maps, Euro centric history books – Why is Christ always depicted as a white man, even though he was living in the Middle East? You get my gist?"

"Yes, you've got a point," said Dwayne shrewdly, "but how can you effect change in a system that you refuse to be a part of?"

"True ... true ..." Wesley's words trailed off. He thought for a moment. "Do you think some sort of positive discrimination within this system would help to redress the balance then?"

"No," was the simple response from his brother. "That only breeds resentment ..." he stumbled on "for everyone to benefit we need a system that rewards hard work, not colour."

"Some would say that having been discriminated against for so long positive discrimination is simply redressing the balance," persisted Wesley.

"I understand what you're saying, Wesley, and I understand why some black people feel that way, but that doesn't make it right, does it?"

Wesley pursed his lips and nodded, "I think you're going to make an okay teacher, bro."

"Well, we'll see," grinned Dwayne. "I've got to get on the course first."

6

The pale buff envelope with Dwayne's name on it sat on the mat in front of the door. He stooped down and picked it up gingerly. It had the London frank on it. It was either a letter of acceptance for interview, or rejection. Dwayne slipped his index finger under the envelope flap and ripped it open. The letter was from Goldsmith's, the address and logo were visible at the top of the paper. Hardly breathing Dwayne unravelled the sheet.

"Yesss ..." He had been asked for an interview.

"Interview, right?" smiled Quisha, as she stumbled down the stairs still looking half asleep.

"Well done!" Hyacinth shouted from the kitchen.

Dwayne rushed excitedly back up the stairs.

"Wesley you awake yet?"

"If I wasn't, I am now," came the reply.

"Can I borrow your grey interview suit?" asked Dwayne, still clutching the letter.

"Sure," chortled his brother, "sure."

Dwayne sailed back down the stairs feeling ready to satisfy his more immediate appetite. His stomach gurgled as he poured himself an extra large helping of muesli. Quisha had just put on Michael Jackson's *Bad* album and it was now filtering throughout the house.

"Ow! I'm bad," sung Dwayne as he moved toward the living room with his bowl of cereal, oblivious to his inaudible tones. Quisha turned up the volume on the hi-fi system.

"Lard, turn it down, for heaven's sake – my head kyan't teck it!" came Hyacinth's voice from the kitchen. "The youth of today!" she hissed under her breath.

By now Quisha was gyrating her body to the grinding base line of her favourite artist, her arms flying in the air.

"Move it, Sis, move it," cracked Dwayne, who was by now caught up in the gyrations of his own body, the cereal bowl balanced precariously in his left hand. He asked his sister wryly, "Who's bad?"

She flicked a glance over to him and smiled.

Thirty minutes later Dwayne was on the phone to Pete, but there was no answer at the other end, so he called Lisa on the off-chance she was in. Since finding herself a steady boyfriend over the summer vacation, her interest in her tech course and, more importantly, him seemed to have dwindled. He let the phone ring three times ..... although it was only nine o'clock in the morning, Dwayne wondered if she had already left for college. On the fourth ring Lisa answered.

"Hi," enthused Dwayne, "how's it going?"

"Oh, hi ya," came the weak voice. "I'm always late on Mondays so whatever it is you'll have to make it quick."

"I've been asked for an interview at Goldsmith's next Thursday." Dwayne was rambling with excitement, oblivious to her cool response.

"That's great," she replied with a little more enthusiasm. "One more obstacle out of the way, anyway."

"Yep," retorted Dwayne. "Hey, I never seem to see you these days, how about meeting up for a coffee in town – Clowns, your favourite?"

There was a short pause on the other end.

"I'm sorry Dwayne but I'm kind of tied up right now, can I call you back on that?"

"Sure," said Dwayne, trying not to sound disappointed. "Give me a call."

He hung up. That girl's doing my head in, he thought to himself, with a slight frown giving him away. He quickly tapped out Pete's number again. It rang twice and his friend droned into the phone,

"Hi."

"Hi Pete, how's it going? Thought you might have been at work, but then I couldn't remember whether you were on the late shift or not."

He didn't bother to tell him that he had rung earlier.

"No I'm on late's ... all this week, I was up to my elbows till two this morning."

"What, did I wake you up then? Sorry about that."

"No worries," came his friend's reply. "How are you then?"

"Pretty good, I just had a letter from Goldsmith's asking me to an interview."

"Ah, good luck mate, when is it then, this interview?" Pete sounded more awake now.

"Next Thursday at ten."

"Gives you a chance to psyche yourself up," chuckled Pete.

"That's right," Dwayne chuckled back. "Hey Pete, can you meet me later on today for a coffee?"

"Sure," replied his friend, "but I'll have to get back by four the latest - you know, to sort myself out for work."

"Okay then, we can meet early ... let's say one?"

"Sounds good to me, usual place, yeah?"

"Just outside Steps," affirmed Dwayne. "See ya later."

Before his friend could reply there was a soft click. Dwayne smiled to himself as he walked away from the phone; at least he had one friend he could depend on. The house seemed quiet now, Quisha had left for work, whilst his mum had gone to help out at the local Oxfam shop on the High Street. Since retiring from the council as a health officer, she found her half-days at the shop helped to keep her sufficiently busy. With Wesley locked in his room, Dwayne decided to wash a few dishes, after which he would study the Goldsmith's prospectus.

Twelve forty seemed to arrive quite quickly. Looking at the clock Dwayne realised that he only had five minutes to spare if he was going to be on time. Knowing that Pete would be punctual he threw down the book that he had been reading for the past hour and dashed upstairs. He looked into his wardrobe and grabbed the blue cotton shorts folded neatly on a shelf. He wondered what he should wear with them. "Hmmm ....." He then waded through a pile of shirts neatly stacked in the top drawer of his dresser. "Bingo." He pulled out a bright white T-shirt with PEPE stamped on the front. Being style conscious Dwayne always liked his clothes to co-ordinate; if they didn't it was deliberate. After all a statement had to be made on occasion. In a flash he was ready.

"See you, Wesley!" he shouted before slamming the front door.

He walked briskly through the side alley that would lead him to the centre of town. Petty Currie was bustling with the midday shoppers. Dwayne dodged a young couple with their floppy sandwiches and cans of coke straight from the shelves of Marks. As he approached the market place he could smell the juice of crushed strawberries – it was wonderful.

"Don't you just love this time of year?" he called to his friend as he approached the entrance of Steps. "The tourists, the strawberries and cream by the river – this is the only time of year when this town is alive."

Pete grinned at him. "Come on, before you burst into song or something."

"Yeah right." They both laughed as Dwayne slapped Pete on the back. Once seated at a coffee table in a dark corner of the basement cafe, Pete stared over at Dwayne and said in a joking manner,

"I'll miss you once you go back to London. I've got used to you rambling on the way you do."

"Ahh – you'll have me crying into my cappuccino in a minute." They both grinned.

"So how's it going with you and … Jenny?" Dwayne winked at his friend, "you two love birds still at the honeymoon stage?"

"Honeymoon stage? No offence Dwayne, but if that was the case, would I be here right now licking this cream cake. Exactly – instead I would be at home licking cream from some erogenous zone."

Dwayne burst into raucous laughter, Pete joined him. Meanwhile an elderly lady next to them started choking on her bagel. At this point Dwayne thought it wise to tone down the conversation.

"Well, are you not giving her enough attention?"

"No, it's not that," Pete's eyes dropped slightly as he shifted in his seat, "we just don't seem to have that much in common when it comes down to it. I like indie while she likes Kylie; I like soya, she likes steak; I like going out, she likes staying in – I mean, need I say any more?"

"Nope, I get the picture," came the sympathetic reply. Dwayne searched for some pearl of wisdom to throw light on his friend's plight, but all he could manage was, "Never mind, these things sort themselves out in the wash."

The ring of truth in this seemed of some solace to his mate who responded with a warm smile. This seemed a good time to leave.

"Hey, let's go grab some ice cream down by the river … yeah?"

"Okay Dwayne, but as long as you're paying," Pete's tone was droll as he pushed his seat backward with both feet.

"That depends on whether or not they're having a sale," said Dwayne, smiling at his own tired joke.

Once more in the narrow streets which characterised Cambridge, the two friends jostled in between the tourists and sightseers heading for the river. Intermittently they stopped to admire quaint objects in quaint shop windows. A stiff breeze was blowing by the time they reached the riverbank, adding movement to the striped canvas that was shading a buxom ice cream vendor. Pete ribbed his friend as if to say she's for you.

"Shame you're already hitched," said Dwayne slyly. Turning on the charm Dwayne then asked the young lady for a double offering of cornetto. With equal charm she handed him the cones whilst taking the money simultaneously. They headed for a bench shaded by a large willow.

"The Raybans are out in force today," observed Dwayne who was now ready to take the conversation down a more trivial path.

"What was that?" asked his friend turning to face him with black Raybans now fixed firmly to his nose.

7

Dwayne woke with a start.

"Seven ... already," he groaned to himself. Squinting he leapt from his bed – he knew that he couldn't afford to be late for his interview. Thursday seemed to arrive quicker than usual which made Dwayne feel slightly unprepared for the day. Once dressed, he slipped down the stairs quietly so as not to wake anyone. Scanning the food shelves, Dwayne reached for the Shreddies box.

"This should make a change," he mused to himself. He crunched the small squares hungrily whilst watching the time nervously. Ten minutes later he was giving himself the once over in the full length mirror on his wardrobe door.

"You handsome devil," he said to himself quietly as he grinned into the glass, pulling the skin tight over his high cheek bones. Such self-adulation always helped to make him feel more confident, although fears of developing into a narcissist loomed in the back of his mind. He checked his watch again, "Eight – running to schedule," he thought aloud. Fifteen minutes later he was on the fast train to King's Cross.

Outside the interview room Dwayne found seven other people waiting; he smiled meekly. They smiled back wryly as if to say, take a hike buster, we don't need any more competition; or so he thought. The atmosphere was tense, nerves were taught. A sneeze broke the silence. The young lady responsible looked around apologetically, the gold buttons on her blazer sleeve glinted as she put a handkerchief to her nose. Dwayne was getting up the nerve to say something to her when the interview door swung open. A distinguished grey-haired gentleman stood in the doorway.

"We all here then?" He turned not waiting for an answer. "Come on in please."

Everyone jostled for the chairs on the periphery of the room, not wanting to take centre stage. Dwayne was bemused, he had not expected a group interview. Feeling unnerved, he sat braced against his seat; he could feel a tension in his bowel. 'All I need do now is fart and totally embarrass myself, thought Dwayne uneasily. Just when my whole future is hanging in the balance.' Dwayne tensed his butt in an effort to counter any inappropriate action that would only serve to further undermine his confidence. The interview began.

"My name is Roger Lowe. First of all I would like to ask you, Dwayne, what you think you have to offer teaching?"

Dwayne smiled meekly into Roger's face in an attempt to look more relaxed.

"Well, first of all I feel that I can understand ... and ummm ... ummm ..." Now his brain was threatening to join in the conspiracy with his bowel by switching off. "Relate to teenagers," stumbled Dwayne. "I can ah ... listen to people and I have confidence in my subject." He crossed his legs as another fart threatened to escape.

"Fine," responded Roger, cutting Dwayne short. "And now the same question to you, Laura." Roger twisted slightly in his seat to face the young lady more squarely. His voice drifted in and out as Dwayne battled with himself. "And now you, umm ... yes, Katie." Roger's voice trundled along at a breezy pace. "Another question for you Dwayne, (there was a pause) I see here on your application, that you failed your 'O' level English and had to do a retake ... what happened there?"

Dwayne was sweating visibly now. "Well, I didn't feel well at the actual exam," said Dwayne evenly, "so I didn't do well, but I did work for it. At least I feel more able to empathise with those who have fears of failing or have failed in the past ... I guess." Dwayne felt that he was now finding his feet.

The interview ended abruptly with, "Well I'm pleased to say that I can offer you all a place on the PGCE course and I hope that your time with us will be both productive and rewarding."

Dwayne shook the hand that was offered to him, a wave of relief sweeping his brow. He was a step closer to his goal. Perhaps he could now have a conversation with the rather friendly-looking girl who had sneezed earlier. He turned around to find her smiling at him, he smiled back.

"Well, we're in," she said.

"Yep ... umm can I buy you a celebratory drink or are you in a hurry?" enquired Dwayne with a subtle nervous edge to his voice.

"Oh no, a drink would be nice. So you're Dwayne ... right?" Her friendly green eyes glistened at him.

"Right. And you are Mandy, if my memory serves me right," he smiled. His tone was much more confident now. They walked toward the sign saying Student's Union.

Once seated, coffees in hand, Dwayne felt relaxed and bubbly.
"So have you come far this morning, Mandy?"
"Not really," came the slightly sing-song response. "At the moment I live in Camden where I've been running my own stall in the market." She gulped some more coffee.
"Selling what?" prompted Dwayne.
"Oh, my own silk prints and a mixture of other fabrics ... well, printed fabrics from various parts of the world." She paused briefly. "I love the Ghanaian fabrics the most you know ... 'cos of their colour and boldness."
"Me too," added Dwayne; his face lit up with increased interest. "So how long have you been in the market then?" came the next question.
"For about two years now, so I felt it was time for a change ... you know."
Dwayne knew.
"So what about you, where are you coming from?"
Dwayne wasn't sure if she meant this in the right on sense, or the geographical, so he guessed.
"Ahh ... Cambridge, I'm staying there with my mum at the moment, you know, and my sister and brother. I was working for a law firm in West London up until early summer but I got fed up with it."
Mandy smiled. "Well this seems like a nice place ... "
Dwayne nodded in agreement. There was a long pause as the conversation waned; both of them felt tired. To save any embarrassing silence Dwayne gulped down the last of his coffee.
"Well, thanks for the chat," he said rather clumsily.
"Thanks for the drink," said Mandy in quick response. They both parted in a cordial manner, both feeling pleased at having made a friend so soon.

Sunday the twenty-seventh of September had finally arrived, the day on which Dwayne was to move into his new digs in Camberwell. He had decided to go for college halls where there was more opportunity to meet people. He had become used to living at home again; to Quisha's constant companionship and understanding; his deep discussions with his brother Wesley (when visiting); and his mum's fussing (which was her way of showing she cared in spite of their recent falling out). Dwayne sighed with a heavy heart. Zipping up the last holdall he marched down the stairs.

"Well, time to go folks," he said cheerily. "I can see the taxi pulling up now."

Hyacinth kissed her son with some affection but in a somewhat reserved manner, wishing that she could understand him; that she could accept him without hindrance, in spite of the homophobic community she had grown up in. Though it was rarely talked about in her day, anyone known to be homosexual was seen as mentally sick. Young boys were warned of such people lest they be taken unawares. Indeed, homosexuals were seen as more of a threat to the community than any heterosexual rapist. How was she now to deal with having a social outcast as a son? How much responsibility lay at her feet? The questions kept pounding inside her head.

Dwayne turned to his sister; they hugged each other warmly before kissing on the cheek. The horn sounded from the awaiting cab. Dwayne slapped Wesley on the back briskly (knowing that a hug would be out of the question – not macho enough).

"Give us a call when you're back in London, bro!" called Dwayne as he strode out toward the taxi, laden with luggage.

8

The first day of college started just as Dwayne expected. Strangers pushed past each other, anxious to get to the correct lecture room at the correct time; programme in hand. Dwayne looked at his own programme – Art Department, Room 30. He went toward the stairs. A good-looking white guy flanked him on his left, Dwayne could not help but to turn his head in order to get a better look. His usual discreet look out of the corner of his eye wasn't enough. The young man smiled before turning off down an adjoining corridor.

Damn, thought Dwayne to himself. Why couldn't he have been going to the same lecture. Oh well, maybe I'll bump into him later ... I hope. Dwayne began to ascend the concrete stairs. A pretty Japanese girl was coming down the stairs in the opposite direction. Long black hair cascaded over her oval face. Her black roll-neck and blue jeans met snugly around her small waist.

"Excuse me, could you direct me to the Art Department?" he blurted out impulsively.

"'Fraid not," she smiled, "I'm looking for the Language Department myself."

"Well ... sorry I can't help you there either." Dwayne grinned at her, displaying a slightly crooked row of teeth; he wanted to hold her there, to continue the conversation, but words failed him. He was feeling slightly uneasy. The young woman looked ready to move on, when Dwayne said clumsily, "Ahh ... so what's your name? Mine's Dwayne." He was now feeling angry with himself for feeling so awkward.

"I'm Candice," her dark eyes held him to the spot, as they smiled with her pert red lips. "Hey, I think we're blocking traffic here," she observed. "How about we continue this conversation at break time – shall we say in the canteen?"

"Sure," said Dwayne quickly. "See you. Bye," he called as she rushed off. 'Wow, what a gorgeous-looking girl', thought Dwayne to himself, 'and she fancies me ... I think'.

The introductory lecture washed over Dwayne as his thoughts drifted to Candice; those luscious lips, the deep brown eyes and that great smile. He looked at his watch – only fifteen minutes to go, he could feel his heart racing. "The next year is going to be very demanding." came the lecturer's voice. His voice drifted out again as Dwayne searched for a mint to freshen his breath. Then he remembered, he had eaten the last one on the train yesterday.

"Damn," he murmured under his breath.

"Right then, see you all tomorrow." came the voice.

Dwayne got up and swiftly made for the exit. He was feeling nervous as he made his way down to the canteen, but at the same time a surge of excitement propelled him down each flight of steps. When Dwayne reached the canteen there was a long line of people stretching around the coffee counter. He urgently scanned the line for Candice, but there was no sign of her. He scanned the seating area – still no joy; he joined the queue. I wonder if she'll turn up, doubts were beginning to trouble his mind. Dwayne checked his watch; five minutes of the break had already gone. The queue edged forward and Dwayne reluctantly moved with it until he reached the selection of cakes and crisps by the checkout. He leaned over for a packet of cheese and onion crisps.

"Hi Dwayne," came a familiar voice behind him. He spun around to find Candice standing in front of him beaming confidently.

"Hi, can I get you something?" Dwayne tried to sound cool, whilst the sensation of relief passed through him.

"A tea please," she replied sweetly.

Dwayne could feel his heart begin to race again, hormones were screaming for release. He noticed for the first time that she wore a delicate gold bracelet which brought out the rich golden hues of her skin.

"How was your lecture then?" enquired Candice once they had sat down.

"Okay I guess," said Dwayne casually, "but it dragged on a bit toward the end – you know how it is. What about yours?"

"Hmmm ... pretty good," she responded, taking the polystyrene tea cup from her lips. "The lady had a sense of humour which helped to keep us interested ... you know."

"Oh, right," was all that Dwayne could offer. "So where are you from?" asked Dwayne.

"South London," she replied, "Clapham area."

"Were you born there then?" Dwayne's tone was inquisitive.

"That's right, but my parents are Japanese."

"I'm British also." This common thread enthused Dwayne to open up further. "My parents came over during the sixties, from Jamaica." Dwayne felt clumsy again, did Candice want to hear this? He looked at her calm face then continued, "Also, we lived there for a couple years when I was a teenager ... ah ... and now we visit when we can so we keep in touch with the relatives ... you know. We were there this summer actually; I really miss the sunshine and food ... and the beach life." Dwayne was rambling now and checked himself. Candice took this cue.

"I feel like that about Japan when I visit. But having said that I couldn't really fit into the culture. Living in a place and visiting are always quite different anyway, aren't they?"

"Yep, that's true," nodded Dwayne, "so ... true ..."

He was drifting into his own personal world, his words trailed off. He imagined the horrors of living in a place where he would be branded as a 'BATTY MAN': he imagined the horrors of being discovered with a man, even; the horrors of being disowned by disgusted relatives; the horrors of being spat on and cursed or even worse ... the horrors of being destroyed ... ever so slowly, by a group of people you had once been proud to call your own, not necessarily by stones or by the gun, but by cold, heartless ignorance. How ironic to be dispossessed by a people who had themselves been dispossessed not so very long ago. The cruel irony punctuated Dwayne's thoughts. His face dropped visibly as he attempted to push these ugly thoughts from his head. He felt old buried feelings once more rising from deep within him. Feelings of alienation, hurt and anger. Paradoxically, whilst in Jamaica he had successfully blocked out all of this. But of course he hadn't gone there to live.

"Are you okay Dwayne?" Candice wrinkled her brow with concern.

"Ahh ... yeah ... sorry, something popped into my head."

"Oh." Her face took on a more inquisitive manner now as Dwayne stumbled for words.

"Yeah, nothing to worry about," he tried to sound casual now, to throw her off the scent. He was not yet ready to trust this sweet stranger with all his secrets. It was enough for now that he felt more at ease with her; he took another sip of piping hot peppermint tea. The conversation carried on for another few minutes and then it was time to move on to the next lecture.

"Well, thanks for the tea, maybe I'll see you later." Candice rose.
"Yeh ... sure ... that's cool," these words were delivered with a definite drawl so as to give his voice a calm seductive edge. He didn't want to give too much away at this stage, after all one had to play the game.

9

The following day Dwayne was keenly scanning the canteen. Surely he would see Candice. Time was wearing on and he had already reached the checkout but still no sign. He paid for his coffee and then found a seat in a very open spot facing the main entrance to this student hang-out. That way he could see everyone entering or leaving the hall; plus Candice would have no trouble spotting him. With only five minutes to go Dwayne was beginning to feel restless and anxious. 'Shit, maybe I played it too cool, maybe I should have made more of a concrete date; date, maybe that's getting too heavy'. Dwayne got up to go to his next lecture feeling somewhat let down. He left bits of torn up polystyrene on the table where he had been sitting as he went off toward the exit.

Another hour's lecture soon passed and Dwayne's thoughts were then brought back to Candice, although he had been successful in shutting her out for the past hour he could keep it up no longer. Besides he was hoping that she would turn up at the canteen for her lunch. Dwayne was to be disappointed once again as he limply held on to a cheese and coleslaw sandwich whilst staring acutely at every person who came through the swing doors.

"That will be ninety pence please, love." Dwayne was pulled out of his trance by the lady who was now holding out her hand for his money.

"Right," he dug into his jeans pocket and pulled out a pound. "Thank you," he said politely as he took his change and shoved it into the same pocket. He went to sit at a table slightly set back from his vantage point of the previous day but nevertheless his view of the exit was still relatively good. He suddenly felt somewhat naked and alone sitting on his own. Everyone else seemed to be busily chatting to their new found friends and colleagues. The large food hall was filled with the drone of many voices talking at once. Dwayne took a bite from his sandwich and chewed with the reluctance of a man on trial. He felt as though he was now lost in this sea of faces with no-one to anchor him. There was a tap on his shoulder, interrupting his thoughts.

"Hi Dwayne! How's it going? Are you going to the tutorial this afternoon?" It was a fellow student, a burly black man that he recognised from one of his lectures. He had only said 'Hello' in passing and certainly couldn't remember his name.

"Oh, hi ... "

Thursday had come and still no sign of Candice, Dwayne was beginning to feel fretful now. He felt as though someone up above was playing games with him, raising his hopes only to have them dashed. He sat staring at his polystyrene cup filled with peppermint tea. Some other students sat at the table making conversation but Dwayne made no effort to become involved. One girl opposite him started to bubble over with laughter, then the others joined in. Dwayne felt miserable, even resentful of his fellow students who were clearly having a good time. Dwayne took another swig of hot tea before getting up to go to the toilet.

"See you later Dwayne," called one of the students at the table.

"Sure," said Dwayne indifferently. He moved towards the exit in a daze.

"Hi Dwayne." Candice pushed back the door almost hitting Dwayne in the face with it. "How's it been going?" she enquired calmly.

"Umm ... okay I guess." Dwayne's eyes were wide, drinking in the sight of the person who had caused him such distress but now filled him with such joy. Inside he was ecstatic but on the outside he managed to conceal this. "I was just about to leave, but I can sit and have a coffee with you."

"Oh, that would be nice," said Candice casually. Her whole manner was summed up by the word casual. She idled up to the coffee counter, swinging her hips energetically. Dwayne followed earnestly, taking a piss would have to wait. Jees, I had better calm down or else she'll think I'm a jerk, thought Dwayne to himself as he continued to battle with his excitement. Just play it cool. They both sat down at a vacant table virtually opposite the cash register.

"Hey, would you like to check a club with me, Saturday night?" blurted out Dwayne quite suddenly.

Candice pouted her lips for a moment. "Sounds good to me," came the reply as her face lit up. "Let's finalise the details on the phone tomorrow, yeah? Here's my number." She pushed a scrap of paper over to Dwayne's side of the table. By now his bladder was bursting and he was in danger of being late for an eleven thirty seminar.

"I've got to go now, but I'll speak to you later okay? See ya." His hand touched her arm as he rose to go.

"See ya," said Candice in a sing-song sort of way.

Friday had come, at last the week was over and the weekend beckoned. Dwayne lay back on his bed and closed his eyes. This first week had taken its toll. A long deep sigh was released from Dwayne's lungs as he allowed the tensions out. He crawled under the covers inviting sleep to take over his weary limbs; his mind however was not willing to co-operate. As it reeled he tossed and turned. He kept evaluating the events that had crammed into such a small space of time. God how he needed the love of a woman; it had been so long since he had kissed a girl or even felt this way about the opposite sex. He felt once again like an adolescent on a first date. Excited, open, vulnerable, and frightened all at once. How could he possibly sleep? How could anyone sleep in this state? He stroked his dick – he hoped that a wank would release some of the pent up energies and help him sleep. He rubbed it back and forth trying to block out all thoughts not of a strictly sexual nature. Both men and women entered into his world of fantasy; for he needed the love of a man as well as that of a woman. However, Dwayne was not yet ready to explore those needs outside of his own personal world. He was not yet ready to fight against the wrath of convention; of society. He let out a cry of relief, as the floodgates opened. Pleasure rippled through his body – now he could sleep.

10

It was Saturday night and Dwayne had a date.
"I feel good!" he screeched, whilst at the same time trying to sculpt his hair into a sharp wedge at the front of his scalp. He peered into the small square mirror that hung over the small white sink in the corner of his room.
"That will do," he said aloud, grinning at his reflection in the glass. "You sure are one sexy guy." He was feeling good and intended to make the most of it. He fastened the small gold buttons on his black silky waistcoat, grabbed his jacket and then stepped out. On his tube journey to Piccadilly Circus he thought about Candice. "Candice, what a beautiful name," he mumbled. No-one took any notice. He thought again about his first week at Goldsmith's. It was now that he realised how little he had conversed with the other students within his department; within the college for that matter. Michael, Jonathan, Julie, Nathan and Diane were the only names that he could recall. His friend, Mandy, had vanished from his thoughts up to now – he had not seen her since the interview. He crossed his legs, shut his eyes, and pushed himself back into his seat, relaxing for the rest of the journey.
Once off the train Dwayne pushed his way past the crowd of people blocking the fast lane of the up escalator.
"Excuse me, excuse me!" he called as he raced up the steps. He could see Candice waiting for him on the other side of the ticket barrier. "Only five minutes late," he panted, "how's that for timing?"
"Not bad," she smiled and gave him a peck on the cheek. "So have you been to Legends before?" she enquired.
"Yep and it's real funky ... I think you'll like it."
"Woo ... sounds promising," she cooed. They walked along Regent Street, arms linked at the elbows. As they approached the club, music could be heard pounding behind the doors. They lined up with the other party revellers. Once inside Candice took off her jacket at the cloakroom revealing a black lycra dress with a cut away back and a small dragon shaped diamonté brooch threatening to crawl down her cleavage. As if in acknowledgement Dwayne stripped off his jacket revealing his black waistcoat over his well-defined torso. It

was like making a statement that he wasn't afraid to show some skin either.

Bright lights reflected off the chrome and stainless steel fittings that gave this club it's modern chic. Dwayne and Candice pushed their way through the sea of young, sweaty faces, animated and vibrant. The music pounded their ear drums as they got on to the crowded dance floor.

"I dig your perfume!" shouted Dwayne above the music.

"Thanks!" Candice shouted back. "You smell pretty good yourself!" Her eyes lit up in a raunchy manner. Dwayne ran his fingers through her long hair as they undulated to the Balearic beats of the music. His hand fell to her small waist; her body was sensuous and her movements provocative. By now sweat was glistening on both their foreheads and the dance floor was becoming increasingly packed. Dwayne flashed a smile at Candice; he was having the time of his life. A bright spot light caught his partner's teeth as she grinned back. By the fifth track Dwayne was beginning to flag.

"Do you fancy a drink?" he mouthed to Candice.

"Yes please," she mouthed back, "but I'm paying," she said in a normal voice as she cupped her lips to Dwayne's ear. They made their way off the floor. Once sitting comfortably at the bar sipping their soda water Candice launched into a discussion about the pros and cons of dating older men. This then led Dwayne to reveal the fact that he sometimes thought about dating women significantly older than himself. This he put down to idolising Diana Ross when a youngster. They both found this thought amusing.

"You're a scream," Candice blurted out in a delayed fashion.

For some reason Dwayne felt awkward and a little shy when she said this. He didn't quite know why. He turned to face the dance floor again. Madonna's 'Erotica' had the dance floor rocking. The words, "I'm a love technician," intoned through the speakers.

"Let's go," said Candice grabbing Dwayne's hand wildly. The night rocked on ...

11

Two weeks and three dates later, Dwayne found himself with Candice in an inexpensive restaurant in China town. The poor service was balanced by the good food and nice company. Dwayne was fighting with his chopsticks whilst trying to convey an air of expertise. Candice looked on quietly confident that her friend would down his meal by the end of the night, albeit a good few hours later. Tonight Dwayne was feeling romantic and slushy. Boy, Candice was something else. He felt that this was so right, he could completely open up to Candice without feeling strange, vulnerable, or even embarrassed. He had talked to her about childhood fears and joys, whilst she shared her experiences of adolescent insecurities interwoven with parental rebellion. As they came to the end of their meal the intensity, in terms of eye contact, increased between them ever so subtly. Candice asked for the bill.

"Let's go dutch," suggested Dwayne.

"Okay," said Candice softly. They paid quickly, then made their way on to the busy streets.

"So where to from here?" asked Dwayne.

"Hmm ... how about my place for a coffee?" suggested Candice.

"Sounds good to me." Dwayne squeezed Candice's hand as they continued along the crowded streets of Soho. She returned the pressure on his hand and then turned to smile at him. The flat she rented was cheap and self-contained; a friend of hers worked for an agency specialising in housing minority women. Having reached Leicester Square tube station, Dwayne felt a irresistible urge to pat Candice on the ass. This he did by allowing her to go in front of him as they descended down the stairs toward the station barriers. She turned ever so slightly and winked as they continued their descent. They both walked briskly through the barriers, tickets in hand. Dwayne could feel a strange sense of excitement creeping over him. The pre-randy stage; the anticipation of things to come. A part of him was still feeling cautious though. After all he hadn't been invited for more than a coffee, or had he? He was still feeling his way in a situation that was new for him. The questions were flying around his head, should he make the next move or would that be too much? He continued to smile at Candice as they sat opposite each other on the tube. He didn't know what else to say or to do at this stage and he definitely didn't want to blow things at this point.

"Are you okay?" asked Candice softly as they got off at Finsbury Park.

"Sure," said Dwayne.

He held on to her hand again as they climbed the steps to the entrance where a lady who looked positively comatose inspected tickets. A few minutes later they were in the street where Candice lived, Bateman Street. This was emblazoned on Dwayne's mind – he hoped to be seeing much of this street in the future, not that he had to let others in on this. Finally, the key turned in the lock of Candice's front door.

Her's was the flat on the ground floor of a converted Victorian terrace.

"Come on in." She tugged at Dwayne's jacket sleeve playfully. "Here let me have your jacket." Being a little nervous Dwayne fumbled with the jacket buttons longer than necessary. The sudden urge to pee didn't help matters any. "Just feel at home," said Candice, beckoning to a simple black and white striped settee. "I'll just go get those coffees."

Dwayne glanced around the neat lounge. There was a black bookshelf against the wall with a ceramic pot on the top shelf and books on those lower down. A beautiful metallic figurine graced the corner opposite the bookshelf. Apart from a rather expensive looking midi next to the shelf, there was nothing else in the room.

"How do you like your coffee?" shouted Candice from the kitchen.

"White with no sugar, please!" Dwayne called back.

"You can turn the hi-fi on!" Candice called out.

"Thanks!" Dwayne got up and went over to the centre. After studying the buttons he managed to get KISS FM on the radio. They were playing blues and soul on the midnight hour. By now Dwayne's bladder was pressing him to go to the toilet. This, mingled with his growing anticipation of sex, was giving him a hard on. He felt that a tactful and rather speedy retreat to the toilet was called for here. When he came out of the bathroom, he found Candice reclining on the settee, mug in hand.

"Here you are," she said, patting the seat next to her. Her legs were crossed in the tight, faded blue jeans that she now had on.

Dwayne reached for the mug on the table before sitting down. His nerves started playing him up again. The pit of his stomach went queasy and his neck went stiff. In an attempt to relax, he took a gulp of coffee.

"Jesus that's hot!" he spluttered.

Candice laughed. Somehow Dwayne felt more at ease now. He put the coffee gingerly down by his feet, then looked into Candice's eyes. She smiled, then put her mug down. Their lips met, delicately brushing against each other. Slowly Dwayne could feel instinct taking over and the tension dissipating. Their breathing became heavier as their tongues searched hungrily. Dwayne squirmed around so that he now lay on top of Candice. His fingers were now caressing her locks as he enjoyed the wetness of her mouth.

"Ummm ... " came the low tones from Candice, before she pulled away from Dwayne. "Let's go into the bedroom, it's more comfortable," she purred.

"Sure." As she pulled Dwayne by the hand, he could feel his dick growing erect; this time he felt no need to hide it. Candice pushed him down on the bed and began grappling with his top. Dwayne pulled her to him wanting to taste her again. He let out a slow groan as their tongues touched again. The sensation of her wet lips against his made him rock hard.

"Ummm ... not bad," said Candice jokingly, as she moved her hand over Dwayne's crutch. Candice was herself feeling ravenous and somewhat turned on by the fact that Dwayne allowed her to take the lead. She liked a man who was not threatened by her, not antagonised by her sense of control. She sensed that Dwayne was a man firmly in touch with his female side having no need for male bravado. She revelled in the sense of freedom that he now gave her. Few men had done this for her. She drank him in as her body secreted it's own juices. Dwayne's breathing now became more rapid as he moved his lips on to the left side of Candice's rather slender neck. Now it was his turn to grapple with her top as he hurriedly tugged at the small studs fastening it together at the front. With no bra on her breasts lay bare. Cupping them with his hands, Dwayne began to massage them whilst instinctively moving his mouth down to her left nipple. His pelvis moved against her as he started to suck her gently. Candice quivered with arousal as the foreplay intensified. She wanted this moment to last for ever. Again her body quivered as

Dwayne's tongue now traced a small circle around her pert nipple ... a small moan escaped from her lips. She pulled back.

"Hey, I've got rubbers in the bathroom," she whispered into his ear.

"Better still I've got some in my back pocket." Dwayne smiled, then sunk his tongue back into her mouth.

"Mmmmmm ... came the low moan as he drank her in.

The sweet smell of Candice's body was the first thing that Dwayne noticed as his eyes opened the following morning. The smell greeted him like the warm smell of honey on toast.

"Hiiii ... " said Candice who was already awake.

"Hiiii ... " responded Dwayne, smiling lazily. "What's for breakfast?" His right hand moved over to stroke her naked body gently.

"W-e-ll, that depends on just how hungry you are," she crooned.

They both chuckled lightly with this subtle innuendo.

"I'll have to think on that," said Dwayne after a few minutes. At the moment it felt good just to lie there stroking her moist skin. This was someone he was really getting into. He pulled her to him for a cuddle. The warmth of her breath was against his neck. Somehow he felt secure, a type of security he hadn't expected. With this woman in his arms he could feel safe in an otherwise unsafe world. They lay in that position for what seemed ages.

"H-e-y, how does warm toast and jam sound?" said Candice finally, as she pulled herself away from Dwayne.

"Great." His tone of voice was woozy.

"Good." Candice flashed her white teeth as she eased herself out of the bed. Dwayne eyed her from behind as she sauntered off to the bathroom. Dwayne felt exquisitely relaxed as he shut his eyes again, a smile spreading over his face. About fifteen minutes later Candice came back from the bathroom. "Come on sleepy head, up you get."

Dwayne let out a slow groan.

"Why not come back to bed?" he responded, eyes still shut.

"I don't think so, lover boy, half the day is nearly gone already and I'm meeting a friend for a coffee in about an hour."

"Oh." Dwayne had been so engrossed with his thoughts that he hadn't stopped to think about plans for the day. In fact, he would

quite easily have cancelled any previous plans in order to spend the day with Candice.
"Don't go all sulky on me now."
"I'm not!" Dwayne snapped, he hadn't been aware of the frown on his face.
"So-rry," whined Candice. "I was only trying to say that it's getting late, that's all." She walked out of the room with her towel still wrapped around her body. Grudgingly Dwayne got up and headed for the shower. The sound of Candice rattling plates in the kitchen, mingled with the sound of running water as Dwayne steamed away the sweat from the night before. Every pore seemed to tingle from the force of the spray. Returning to the bedroom after ten minutes, dripping wet, Dwayne glanced at the clock on the dresser by the bed. Ten thirty-five showed on the digital display as he hastily jumped into his trousers. A few minutes later and he was munching on buttered toast topped with thick chunks of marmalade. He eyed Candice evenly as she scoffed down a second helping of toast and lean bacon.
"Slow down baby, or you'll give yourself indigestion." Candice ignored him and continued.
"I've decided to go check Camden for some books," said Dwayne trying another tack. "It's always buzzing on a Sunday you know. I might even stop off at the Jazz Cafe for some lunch."
"Sounds good," Candice seemed uninterested, almost distracted.
"Is every thing okay, Candice?"
"Sure, why do you ask?" She got up from her seat quickly, not hanging around for an answer.
Dwayne felt puzzled as she breezed out of the lounge, leaving her greasy plate lying on the floor. Had he done something wrong, said something maybe, why did he feel suddenly awkward? He followed Candice into the bedroom where she was now applying her make-up.
"So when can wee ... ahh get together next?" The words fell out of Dwayne's mouth without any flow.
"Tomorrow after college would be good," Candice replied without turning around.
"Okay then." Dwayne tried not to sound too excited, in case she thought he was too eager. The tone of her voice made him wonder if she was doing the same.

Indeed, Candice was beginning to suspect just that. The almost naive eagerness that Dwayne had shown her the night before had seemed attractive then, but now it seemed cloying. She wondered if he was reading more into her obvious attraction for him than there was. At this stage of her life there was certainly no room for any heavy relationships.

The following day they took a slow walk through Hyde Park, hand in hand.

"Candice, can I ask you something?" blurted out Dwayne, with a nervous edge to his voice.

"Mmmmm ... depends on what it is ... just kidding, go ahead."

"Well, I, or rather we've been seeing each other for a while now and I was, well (the uninvited feelings of awkwardness were creeping up on him again) ... wondering where we ... ah ... go from here. You know, does this mean that you want to take the relationship ... a step further?" There, it was out, Dwayne turned to face Candice. She halted in her stride.

"Oh ... "

A long pause followed. Dwayne's feelings of awkwardness were now giving way to sheer nervousness.

"Listen Dwayne ... uhh ... I thought that we were just good friends who had a good time together ... you know." Candice looked into the confused eyes that stared back at her. "I mean, with work and teaching practice round the corner I didn't think that either of us were looking for a ... for a relationship."

Visibly stunned Dwayne struggled to maintain some face.

"Right, as long as I know where I stand, that's cool."

"I'm sorry if I gave you any mixed signals," continued Candice.

"Let's hit the tube," said Dwayne in as composed a manner as he could manage. He spun on his heels and smartly marched toward Marble Arch tube station. 'What the hell is she saying to me, what the bloody hell is she saying to me?' said Dwayne within his head.

A mixture of thoughts and feelings came to greet Dwayne that night as he lay in bed, unable to sleep. How could he have read Candice so wrong? Why was fate playing such cruel games with his heart? And perhaps the most disturbing thought of all – was he tarnished, somehow flawed, unlovable even? Was he sending out signals that said don't touch – rejected goods? Was that it? Had the years of being slighted by society, disowned by community, and ultimately rejected by family left a rank smell? What was to become of him? Dwayne drew thin shallow breaths – he was scared. His eyes blinked as they grew tired and heavy. But more questions filtered through: Why hadn't he told Candice about his sexuality? Had that been the source of their undoing? Had she been less than satisfied with their lovemaking, aware that a part of him was not open to her? To her who wanted to fill his every space? At least in this analysis he was loveable, at least that.

12

The day had finally arrived when theory was to be put into practice; this was Dwayne's first day of teaching practice. A day that he had been looking forward to, but at the same time dreading. His tutor, Paul, had assured him of these feelings before hand. Dwayne entered the main entrance to Beach School, a mixed comprehensive, on the stroke of eight forty-five. He found his tutor and another colleague waiting patiently in the staff room.

"Ah, good morning Paul, hi Kate."

"Morning Dwayne," came the dual response.

"Nervous?" enquired Paul.

"I'm feeling a little queasy," Dwayne forced a smile.

"Don't worry, we're sending you in with a really nice first year group to begin with." Paul's calm manner immediately put Dwayne at ease. He already had his lessons pre-planned and was as prepared for the day as seemed possible, yet he wondered if there was something, something fundamental that he had forgotten. The bell intruded into his thoughts.

"Well, I suppose it's time." He looked over at Kate. "When is your first lesson?"

"Not until eleven." She smiled weakly. "Gives me a little breathing space – anyway good luck."

"I'll need it," retorted Dwayne, "see you later."

As Dwayne marched toward Room 56 with his tutor, the pep talk continued.

"Now just be yourself in there and remember that I'm in there not only to observe but to help, okay?"

"Okay." Dwayne put his thumb up to reinforce his acknowledgement. As they entered the classroom the pupils sat quietly eyeing both parties with caution. A bit like a family of lions eyeing up their next meal. Paul went to find a seat at the back whilst Dwayne stood in front of the blackboard.

"Good morning everyone! My name is Mr Stevenson and I'm going to be your art teacher for this term." Attentive bright eyes stared back at him. He continued. "Now, first of all I would like to establish with you my rules for the classroom. Everyone get these down off the blackboard please."

Chairs and pens clattered as the pupils readied themselves for what they were about to copy. He had them with him, his stomach eased.

That night Dwayne sat in his room alone, his thoughts wandered from school to his recent talk with Candice – his heart sank.

Two weeks on and the kids were now testing their relationship with Dwayne. He walked down the corridor to his next class. A student called, "Yo sir!" Another, "Touch," hand held out. These were street-wise kids attempting to relate to him on what they thought were his terms. Dwayne turned to address the young man who had offered the last comment.

"Now look young man, do you address other teachers in that manner; no I didn't think so." The boy in question looked bemused. Dwayne moved on swiftly, "I find your manner rather flippant, so please, next time, good morning will do. Okay?"

The pupil nodded and both parties moved on. Dwayne reached his class to find a rather noisy reception awaiting him. It was 9u and already he felt a sinking feeling in his stomach. The honeymoon period was clearly over now and he would need to prove himself not only a competent teacher but a respected teacher in the art of good behaviour.

"9u, line up quietly, please."

So far, so good, thought Dwayne to himself, as they jostled into position.

"Okay, come in quietly please." Dwayne moved to his desk as the kids bundled in through the door; scrambling for the prized seats. 'I'd better give them time to settle down, I suppose,' Dwayne felt the sinking feeling creeping back. Five minutes later Dwayne felt he was losing it. "Quiet please!" He was getting nowhere and the kids smelt blood. Dwayne turned to the blackboard and wrote up the word DETENTION. Quite suddenly noise levels fell – for the moment Dwayne was on top. "Well now, can you get out your sketches from last lesson whilst I take the register." Twenty minutes into the lesson and things were going okay. The still life was still intact, perched on a table in the centre of the room. Dwayne bent over to view a pupil's sketch.

"Twat!" screamed a young girl as she hurled a rubber at a boy opposite her.

"Sir!"

All of a sudden mayhem broke loose as projectiles were sent zinging across the classroom. Dwayne stood up and folded his arms.

"Now stop this immediately!" A paper pellet struck his chest from nowhere. Dwayne was by now getting a tad cheesed off. "The next person to throw anything is going straight to the Head of Department!"

He had gained another respite, Dwayne let out a heavy sigh. Glancing at his watch he wished for a speedy delivery to the lunch break. "9u!" he bellowed; would he have a voice by then??

Later that night Dwayne imagined himself in the arms of Candice. He needed comforting, to be held; the child in him was wanting. These thoughts left him feeling frustrated and, yes, a little angry, he couldn't help it. He lay down on his bed pulling his knees up toward his chest. All the times that he had been hurt seemed to culminate in that one moment. Bile rose to his throat as he tried to pull his knees up further; to resist the grip of despair pulling him under now seemed futile. Random thoughts filled his head, faces from the past pierced his mind. Dwayne swallowed hard as the bile continued to fill his throat. "Hell," he cursed softly under his breath. As he stared at the cream wall in front of him he felt lonely; so very lonely. In an attempt to shut out this feeling he shut his eyes, but still the feeling remained. He thought of his family and the rejection he had received from them, again of Candice. Bitter bile coated his tongue, he swallowed again. Self-pity was now his only friend. As tears streamed down Dwayne's cheeks, he sobbed quietly into his pillow.

13

One day seemed pretty much like another for Dwayne now. During the day he was at school shouting at the kids in order to make himself heard, and then returning home to a never ending stream of marking, evaluation, and lesson planning. Distress and anxiety seemed to dog him in all corners of his life, taunting him, wearing him down. He gasped for air as the muscles in his throat tightened.

Click went the coin box as the money dropped and the connection made between Dwayne and his sister Quisha.
"Hi Sis, how are you doing?" Dwayne tried to sound up beat.
"Oh fine. Me and James are still going strong, but work's kinda tiring me out at the moment. Still better busy than bored, eh?"
"Yeah ... guess you're right there," quipped Dwayne. "Right now it seems as though there aren't enough hours in the day, you know?"
Quisha chuckled lightly down the other end of the line. "How's school?" she asked.
"Pretty crazy," came the low key response. "The kids are wearing me out, you know. I feel as though I'm on a tread mill. In the evening when I get in, I'm still having to lesson plan and mark - so I don't even have a chance to wind down before the next day. I'm even tense right now."
"Oh," came the voice on the other end, "that doesn't sound too cool."
"It's not. My social life stinks .... I don't even have time for a movie right now. Hmm ... then again I don't have anyone to go see a movie with."
"Come on Dwayne, you can always see a movie by yourself," chided Quisha softly; "you are a big boy now."
"Oh, you're funny aren't you," replied Dwayne, irritated by his sister's sarcasm.
"Listen bro, stress is the buzz word right now ... you know ... it's just the way things are (pause) I guess." This more sympathetic tone went some way toward soothing Dwayne's irritation.
"Yeah, I guess you're right," he said somewhat wearily. His voice trailed off. "Hey, enough of me droning on, crumbs I'm

becoming a right old whinger. How's Mum and Wesley doing – okay?"

"Oh sure, Mum's watching some movie on the box right now and Wesley's gone back to the big smoke today, so he'll probably call you later. Hey, I just remembered, I'm going to join an aromatherapy course next week, (pause) you know, as a night class." Quisha's voice was high with enthusiasm.

"Good for you," replied Dwayne, "sounds just up your street," he chuckled. "Hey, I'm going to have to hang up now, I've run out of dosh. Say hi to Mum for me and I'll see you all soon." In his mind Dwayne had wanted to send his love but some how he still felt a little sore at his mum for making a part of him feel unloved.

"Okay, bye," came Quisha's reply as the line was cut.

Hanging up the receiver Dwayne turned to find a cue of irate-looking faces outside the telephone booth. He smiled apologetically as he marched off towards his digs and a pile of books. Once in his room he slipped off his shoes and sat down behind his desk. He thumbed through his diary, counting the weeks to Christmas. In his mind this marked a break from the roller coaster that his life had become. Thoughts were flying around inside his head that he didn't have time to unscramble. Lesson plans and exercise books beckoned with urgency.

An hour later Dwayne was slipping his shoes on again. The telephone conversation with his sister was tugging at his forehead. He knew he wasn't going to get anything done until he'd spoken to Candice. They hadn't spoken for nearly two weeks. He wasn't sure if they could just be friends, he wasn't sure if he could make the adjustment; he needed to try.

Candice smiled enigmatically as she opened the door.

"Hi," she said in her usual casual manner; "Come on in, stranger, I'm on the phone, so just help yourself to juice or whatever."

"Fine," said Dwayne, as he moved toward the kitchen. Moments later the phone went down with a gentle pip and Candice turned to face Dwayne, who was now sharing the settee with her.

"Thought I would see how you were doing." The words came out heavily.

"It's been a little while," said Candice.

"Yeah, I guess, but you know how it is ... with work and teaching practice."

"Right." Candice looked at him with a blank expression. Dwayne stumbled on. "How's it going for you at school?"

"Okay I guess, kind of tiring though." There was a long pause. Candice felt uneasy now, not because of the silence but because she didn't feel relaxed with Dwayne right now and she was sure that her gut instinct to let go of him as quickly as possible would be the best. The hurt that was hiding behind each word that Dwayne spoke; the hurt that now hid behind his tired eyes; were confirmation that they could not stay friends – at least not for now.

"Listen, talking about school, I've still got some preparation to do for tomorrow," continued Candice in the same droll manner.

"Okay then," came Dwayne's curt response. He got up and headed for the door. "Bye."

He closed the door without waiting for a reply. He felt well and truly pissed off as he made his way back to the tube station. He was oblivious to the other night riders who pushed past him on the train, similarly shrouded in their own world. The strained conversation between him and Candice was replaying in his mind. Dwayne realised now that they had come to a dead end. Once more back on the streets Dwayne kicked a coke can along the pavement as he walked aimlessly past his halls.

The following day Dwayne marched through the school gates five minutes early, determined to start the day feeling a little more relaxed. At least he would have time to have a piss before the first bell signalling the start of the day.

"Hi," smiled his colleague, Kate, "you're early."

Her round snub nose and full cheeks had a warm friendly glow.

"Oh, you're funny aren't you!" snapped Dwayne, "It's not as though I'm ever late."

"I didn't mean it that w..." Before she could finish Dwayne turned sharply on his heels heading for the toilet, leaving Kate to walk the rest of the main corridor on her own. As she entered the staffroom laden with her bag of books, she felt confused. She didn't understand why Dwayne had reacted toward her in such a fashion. She hadn't meant anything by what she had said; just making conversation. Still in a quandary she said the routine, "Morning!" in a blanket fashion to the people sitting around the room. A few of them looked up from their cups of coffee.

"Morning," they replied.

Kate edged toward the Max-Pax machine, dropped her bag, then hunted around for change. Moments later she was swilling around the powdery sludge in the cardboard cup whilst glancing over her timetable. She looked up when the door swung open and Dwayne marched in, still looking peeved. Without saying anything he sat down in a chair next to her

"Looking forward to the Christmas break?" she offered casually.

"Yeah ... but I'll still have my second assignment to finish off." came the gruff response.

"Me too," pitched in Katie quickly, "still... " The bell interrupted her sentence. Dwayne got up hurriedly.

"I'm teaching first thing ... see ya." He left the room with the string of bodies now moving toward their classes.

"Okay 8l, get your coats off before going in, please," instructed Dwayne. Each pupil filed into the classroom obligingly. "Quiet now please," he continued calmly.

"Sir, I didn't do my homework because I stayed round my Nan's last night," reeled out a fair-haired girl in glasses.

"I didn't finish it either, sir," came a chorus of voices. Dwayne was already feeling exasperated and the day had only just began.

Barry White's deep baritone voice crooned into Dwayne's ears through the small Sony speakers inserted in each ear. "I love you just the way you are," he sang.

As he lay stretched out on his bed, in blue jeans and a red roll neck sweater, he imagined himself back on that beach in Jamaica, baking in the sand. In this way, for the ten minutes that he had lain down, he had managed to forget the lesson plans and exercise books on the desk; the cold winter air outside; and the misery of being Dwayne. He didn't hear the first knock or the second one, as his Walkman played loudly in his ears. Finally though he heard the third one and switched the machine off.

"Yes!" he shouted, "Who is it!"

"Hi, Dwayne, your brother's on the phone!"

"OH ... okay, thanks!" he shouted back through the thick wooden door. Moments later he was outside on the landing talking to his brother, Wesley.

"Hi! Quisha said you were back in town. How's the Beeb treating you?"

"Fine," said Wesley vaguely, "it's a bit of a slow period at the moment so I can't wait for the holidays. Are you going back home as soon as you break up or hanging around London awhile?" enquired Wesley.

"Going straight home," answered his brother. "I need to just slow down, you know. Why, were you thinking of going clubbing or something?"

"Well, it's a possibility," replied Wesley. "So how's it at school?"

"Oh you mean the madhouse. Could be better, you know. The kids are pretty wild at times."

Wesley laughed into the phone.

"Hey ... " Dwayne was just about to mention his recent fling with Candice but decided against it. There seemed to have emerged from somewhere a mutual understanding between Dwayne and Wesley not to talk about each other's love life just in case men crept into the conversation.

"Yeah, what's that then?" asked Wesley, waiting for his brother to finish the sentence.

"Oh, it's okay, I'll leave it for now ..."

"Okay. I guess I'll see you in a couple weeks then for the festive season or if you've got time we can meet up before."

"Okay," said Dwayne, "bye for now."

"Bye."

The line went dead. Dwayne walked back to his room and closed the door. He lay back down on the bed and replaced the earphones. Barry White's voice faded away; there was a fuzzy sound and then the familiar voice of his father.

"Quisha, you can't go out wearing just a bra – for God's sake, wear some clothes."

"Dad, it's a Gaultier top and it's the fashion." Quisha's voice had an edge of irritation.

"Quisha what do you think ..."

His Dad's voice was cut as the play button flicked up on the Walkman. Dwayne was stunned. To hear his father's voice again so unexpectedly. It played with his sense of reality. For a moment it seemed that his dad was still alive; the voice was as strong as ever. It was almost as though he could go and call him from the next room. Dwayne pulled the tape from the machine and viewed it carefully. It had completely slipped his mind that as a joke he had taped his dad arguing with his sister so as he could play it back to Quisha – the leading fashion guru. He never did. Now he felt haunted by his own design. He felt a longing creep into his heart, a kind of sadness but the time for tears had passed. He chucked the tape into the metal bin beneath his desk forcefully. The cassette cracked and a dull din echoed around the room. This in itself was a telling sign that the time for tears had not passed – he only thought it had.

14

Christmas and New Year came as a brief respite for Dwayne, but all too brief as far as he was concerned. Although he spent much of the time vegetating in front of the TV feeling uncomfortable and bloated, he found it difficult to unwind; it seemed his body had forgotten how to do so. Still, being back at home was nice, with his mum fussing over him and his brother and sister chatting nineteen to the dozen; he could at least attempt to switch off from the past few weeks. His present state of angst had not gone unnoticed as his family had become aware of a terseness in his manner that had not been there before. Hyacinth was convinced that he had lost weight. Still, she was simply glad to have all her children home again – back in the nest.

With the ritual festivities over, Dwayne called his friend Pete to catch up with the latest on his side of the fence. He listened for the ringing on the other end, then the click as Pete answered the phone.

"Hi Pete! Guess who?" he said into the receiver.

"Ah ... hi ya, Dwayne. How are you?" His words sounded stilted. "Long time no hear," he continued in a more even manner.

"Well, you've got my number," said Dwayne defensively. He didn't need this, what the hell's going on here he, thought to himself.

"Okay, okay," replied Pete, "it's just an expression ... Jees."

Dwayne now felt some what sorry that he had called.

Pete also shared this sentiment. How could he explain to Dwayne that he no longer had time for him. That between work and his girlfriend, Jenny, his world was now filled. That in the time he had been away, he and Jenny had worked out their differences and now he felt complete. That he no longer needed his friendship the way he used to.

"How's school going?" he asked in a strained manner.

"Well, to be honest, quite rough really." In his mind this was the last thing Dwayne wanted to talk about. He wanted to talk about their friendship – why Pete was now distant – as he held the receiver he got the sensation of talking to the phone. Still he tried to carry on as though nothing was wrong. "How's work for you? Are you still doing those awkward shifts."

"Mmm ... works fine and with any luck in the new year the hotel's taking on an extra person, so I'll just do days."

"Nice one," said Dwayne enthusiastically in an attempt to rescue the conversation. There was now a silence as both parties struggled for words - words to fill the space that had come between them.

"Well a Happy New Year anyway, Pete," said Dwayne finally.

"Thanks, same to you Dwayne ... Bye."

The phone went click before Dwayne could say bye. He stared at the receiver for a few seconds before putting it down. He knew that another link to his past had been severed. Why was this happening to him? Had he done something in a past life to deserve this? As far as he knew he had always valued his friendship with Pete - always. Again the question came; why was this happening? He drew now on all his inner resources in an effort not to allow the conversation with Pete ruin the last few days of his holiday. Dwayne drank and ate almost continuously now. Somehow this gave him comfort in his ever shrinking world.

Alas, the break was all too short and Dwayne felt a sense of real reluctance now as he once more entered the hallowed halls of education. He now felt resentment for an occupation that had taken over his life. He longed for the rose-tinted spectacles that he once used to own. How much realism could a guy take? The classroom door glided open as Dwayne entered. With only five minutes to the bell he had little time to prepare for his first lesson. The bell rang and the crazed sound of young teenagers could be heard outside in the corridor. The classroom door opened.

"Can we come in sir!"

Dwayne looked up from his desk.

"Yes." Moments later Dwayne was introducing the class to the topic of textures amid a buzz of excitement.

"Jamie, could you stop talking and get on with some work!" snapped Dwayne, halfway through an already trying lesson. The holiday mood was still with the kids and trying to switch them to work mode was proving difficult.

"Oh, fuck off!" came the equally snappy response. The words seemed to reverberate around the room for ages. Dwayne glared at the youngster in shock, the rest of the class stared in silence, waiting for a response. They didn't have to wait for long.

"Get out!" blurted Dwayne. "Go directly to the Head of Department. I'll deal with you later." He felt his composure coming back. "Everyone get on with your work!" Heads went down and remained down for the rest of the lesson. The little shit, thought Dwayne to himself. A fear of failure had gripped him – hard.

In the Departmental Head's office Jamie looked subdued.

"I've told Jamie that a letter is going home and that his Year Head will be dealing further with this matter." His colleague looked reassuringly at him, as if to say, never mind it's all in a day's work.

Marching along the corridor Dwayne made for the staffroom. Seething with anger he felt as though he was about to break into a sweat, but nothing came; what he was actually feeling was the tightness of his scalp as it constricted over his skull. Once he had closed the door of the staffroom behind him he felt the pressure around his head begin to ease. He then began the business of sharing his morning's incident with Kate, who was herself looking rather peeved.

"Did he call you anything racist?" came an enquiring voice from the corner. The male colleague from which the voice emanated looked on inquisitively. Dwayne was stumped. "If he did, we can get rid of him on that," continued the member of staff. "He's abusive to everyone."

If he knew what it was like to be called a nigger; a wog; or a black bastard he would never have asked that question, thought Dwayne wearily, some people just have no idea. He recalled the times that he had been walking home late at night through the quiet streets of Cambridge and a car full of lager louts crawled by, flinging their insults at him with venom and hate. One could only walk on or else hate them back. Dwayne always walked on.

"No, he didn't," retorted Dwayne dryly.

"Are you sure?" pressed the colleague.

"YES." Dwayne turned and walked back out of the door that he had moments earlier walked through. He went in search of someone who could make him feel human again; not a receptacle for abuse; not a teaching machine; not someone devoid of all feelings but a human being.

That evening Dwayne lay on his bed staring at the yellow-stained ceiling. He noticed the way dust had settled around the light bulb and the small spider that was now crawling down from the light fitting. Feeling dejected, lonely and sad, the words, 'I'm not a failure. I'm not a failure' went round and round in his head. His eyes eventually strayed down from the ceiling to the pile of marking he had on his small desk. He sighed heavily.

"Damn it, I'm going out!" he said aloud. With this new thought he jumped up from his resting position. 'Like Quisha says, I don't have to rely on other people'. His thoughts became more lucid, 'It's time I stopped feeling like a victim, feeling sorry for myself. That's it Dwayne, think positive'. He slipped on his shoes, then checked himself in the mirror. It was only once out on the pavement that Dwayne wondered, 'Now where to? Mmm ... there's always something happening down the West End. That will do'. Once on the tube he then made up his mind to see a movie. At least that was something he could do on his own. He didn't quite feel right when he eventually reached the MGM on Tottenham Court Road. Somehow it seemed strange to be walking through the doors on his own. 'God, even the woman at the cash register seems to be looking at me strangely', thought Dwayne, 'she's probably thinking "here's another sad loner"'. Dwayne looked around the foyer where couples and groups chatted whilst waiting for their turn at the popcorn counter. He paid for his ticket then walked into the darkened interior.

To his relief he could see a few single people sitting around the auditorium. He relaxed a little. He decided to go sit next to a middle-aged, Hispanic-looking gentleman who was just a few steps away. Suddenly the auditorium was plunged into darkness as Dwayne tripped over someone's bag immediately before him.

"Oh sorry," he said, instinctively putting his hand out in front of him.

"Eeek!" screeched a lady's voice as his hand landed on her crotch. He could tell from the roundness of her thighs that she was a well-built woman.

"Sorry," he gasped whilst stumbling on.

"Sssshhh ....." hissed people either side of him.

The film dialogue had just started. With some relief Dwayne could just make out the empty seat that he had been aiming for. He plonked himself down with relief. Now he could sit back and enjoy. He glanced at the screen only to see a mass of hair frizzed out in all directions; it seemed aimed, or even conceived, by the owner to upset some poor sucker's view. Dwayne groaned inwardly. Craning his neck he decided to make the best of an awkward situation. About twenty minutes into the film Dwayne's neck began to get stiff, so he leaned over a bit further without thinking about the fact that he was now obscuring some other poor soul's view, not to mention that he was also leaning on the shoulder of the gentleman next to him. A light prod from the person behind jolted Dwayne's senses. He looked behind apologetically, not that the person could see his face in detail or read lips and then to the gentleman who sat by his right shoulder. In the darkness Dwayne could make out the white of his teeth as he smiled across to Dwayne. This somewhat surprised Dwayne as he instinctively smiled back.

The film wore on inanely as far as Dwayne was concerned, as by now he had lost all sense of where the plot was going. He wondered why the guy next to him had smiled, or rather grinned, so deliberately. It seemed out of place. He discreetly glanced over at the guy as this thought continued to hammer in his mind. The guy was looking at Dwayne, the whites of his eyes reflecting brightly in the illumination from the screen. Dwayne snapped his head back to face the screen. He hadn't expected that. He felt uneasy now and a little strange. The movie certainly wasn't failing to engage Dwayne alone. An hour went by without any further incidents; Dwayne kept head and neck firmly fixed ahead.

Finally the credits went up and Dwayne could relax, no more craning. He glanced once again to his right, somehow curious about what reaction he would get, if any, from the man beside him. People either side of them shuffled as the Hispanic guy whispered,

"What a boring film, eh?"

Dwayne smiled into the face of this rather friendly character. 'I wonder, probably a tourist', thought Dwayne to himself. In his experience that would explain the friendly interest. But then again he couldn't be sure.

"I know," whispered back Dwayne. "Still I guess it had it's moments."

They rose with the crowd that was by now preparing to surge toward the exit. Being used to the lack of light, the rows of people began filing out. Dwayne couldn't help noticing how finely chiselled the features of the guy next to him were, how handsome he looked in spite of the tell-tale grey hairs Dwayne had noticed before the film. Their row began to move off. Dwayne turned to move towards his left, when the stranger's voice came to his ear again, but this time louder.

"Can I buy you a drink, or are you in a hurry?"

He hadn't expected this and stammered, "Sure ... but it will have to be quick." 'Hell? why not', he thought, 'better than sitting in my room on my own. I need the company'. They moved out into the crowded West End street – Oxford Street was as busy as ever.

"I know a bar not far from here called The Village – it's got a happy hour on till late," he grinned. "Just one thing though I'm not sure how you feel about this ... it's gay."

Everything clicked into place. Dwayne felt so naive. He thought quickly then said, "Ahhh ... yeah, that's fine." 'What are you doing!' screamed a small voice from inside his head. That little voice that is afraid of society; afraid of what people will think.

15

One drink had turned into two, Dwayne wasn't sure where things were heading but he didn't want them to stop. Feelings that had been pushed under for a long time were now beginning to surface. Not slowly but in a rush. He knew that he wanted to experience sex with a man. 'I wonder what sex with this guy would be like, he's not bad looking at all'. Dwayne smiled into his drink as the dim lights of The Village bar shone through his glass. He felt warm, excited but frightened all at the same time.

'Suppose he wasn't ready for this, hell what about what he had heard about ass fucking ..... would he be expected to do it? Wasn't it dangerous? What if he had made some gross mistake and this guy didn't fancy him at all? What if he made an idiot of himself? What if...?' The thoughts whirled around in his head.

"So what do you do for a living?" asked Viv, by this stage they had exchanged names.

"Oh, I'm a student teacher. My subject's art. What about you, what do you do?"

"Ahhh ... let's just say that I'm in between jobs at the moment." Viv looked slightly embarrassed.

"Oh well, you're not alone there," said Dwayne in a light-hearted tone.

"Huh, believe it or not I was earning good money as a manager not so long ago ... still." His eyes glazed over as he put his bottle of Becks to his lips. Dwayne became more attentive now as the conversation deepened.

"How old are you Viv?" he asked the question in a casual manner.

"Thirty-nine," a pause, "does that bother you?"

"No, why should it?" answered Dwayne defensively. He looked down from Viv's eyes to the glass in his hand. Viv ignored the question, resting his left elbow on the bar. His black faded jeans and woollen sport jacket did his lean frame justice.

"Do you want a coffee round mine?" he asked moments later, making fresh eye contact with Dwayne. Again the small voice screamed inside his head but this time louder. His body felt welded to the bar stool on which he sat. Only now did he take in the many faces surrounding him – the many men eyeing each other up. Only now did his senses fully register the background jazz that permeated the cruisy atmosphere of The Village. Only now did he notice the arty pictures of nude men hanging from the walls. Dwayne's heart thumped against his rib cage. It was now or never, and life was to short for never.

"Okay." Dwayne gulped; he had taken the plunge.

Dwayne sat on the soft leather couch, feeling warm and woozy as the dulcet tones of Janet Jackson oozed sensuality.

"That's the way love goes," she crooned over and over again. He took a sip of his coffee, then turned to face Viv next to him.

"Nice place you've got here." Viv smiled sweetly but said nothing. His eyes and sleek black midi seemed to do all the talking necessary. The simple wall hanging and pine strip floorboards seemed to suit Viv's easy manner. There was an honesty, an openness about him that Dwayne found intriguing. Any uneasiness that remained seemed to be dissipating with each passing minute. The small digital clock on the bookshelf read a quarter to one. Viv put his mug down and started to stroke Dwayne's head, rubbing his soft curls one way then another. Gingerly Dwayne put his mug down. He to began to rub Viv's scalp in a similar fashion. His short cropped hair made it easy for Dwayne to feel the bumps on his scalp.

"That's the way love goes ... " The melody was making Dwayne feel sexy, not that he needed much help.

"That's the way love goes ... " insisted Janet. If Dwayne had anything to say on the matter it was lost in what was now a frenzy of sucking and licking. His tongue was wildly caressing the back of Viv's neck, whilst Viv's tongue did strange things to his ear.

"Mmmmm ... " said Viv withdrawing, "let's carry this on in the bedroom where things are, how should I say it? More comfortable."

"Okay," said Dwayne dreamily, "but let's be clear about one thing, no ass fucking and no cumming in each others mouth ... okay?"

"That's two things," replied Viv with a wry expression. Dwayne waited for more, but nothing more was said. Shit, he must think I'm a real virgin prude. Dwayne felt that somehow, however subtly, a shutter had come down between him and Viv. Minutes later they lay on the bed with renewed vigour, any moments of tension were now dispersed.

"Relax," said Viv softly into Dwayne's ear, "I'm not going to do anything to you that you don't want."

Dwayne felt better, reassured; now he could be really hedonistic, let himself go wild. He pulled at Viv's shirt and belt whilst Viv did the same with his attire. Their lips made slurping sounds as they continued to eat each other up. Once naked Viv drew back.

"Ooooh ... you are one good-looking guy." His eyes scanned Dwayne's body from head to toe. He smiled back at Viv.

"Thanks." His ego did a high jump. Viv got up and walked over to the dresser.

"We're going to party." He turned back around to face Dwayne holding a bottle of baby oil and a tube of lube. His dick was erect. Dwayne lay back, he was determined to enjoy tonight ...

Dwayne woke up the next morning feeling wonderful. He looked over at Viv, who was still sleeping. It was only now that Dwayne noticed the crows feet around his eyes and the deep lines across his forehead. His nose seemed to bend in an awkward manner. Okay, so he wasn't a fashion model but you couldn't have oral sex with someone and not feel a connection, or so Dwayne felt. His eyes glanced around the room scanning the scattered clothing and piles of Kleenex, then he saw the clock.

"Shit!" He bolted upright – he would be late for school. How could I have been so reckless as to sleep over with – with a complete stranger? How could I be so bloody stupid, so bloody thoughtless? He glanced over at Viv, who's nose began to twitch. Oh no, what the hell am I going to do? Panic was setting in. Friday mornings were hard at the best of times, but this beat the cake. He calculated that if he got dressed, skipped the shower and breakfast; he'd still be an hour late. His hand moved down to a sticky dick, skipping the shower was definitely out of the question.

"Viv, are you awake yet?" snarled Dwayne.

"Mmmm ... oh hi," beamed Viv.

"I'm late for school, I'll be crucified. Can I use your phone? I'm going to have to phone in sick."

"Sure, go right ahead," insisted Viv, quite glad for this new development.

Once the call had been made Dwayne eased himself back into the bed. He felt calmer now, more able to disengage from those thoughts that were in any way threatening to his mornings pleasure.

"Crisis over," he said whilst snuggling up to Viv.

"Don't get too comfy," laughed Viv, "I've got to go take a piss ... sorry."

Dwayne grudgingly allowed him out of the bed. He rolled over on to his back and put his hands beneath his head. He felt all slushy and wonderful again. He thought of the night's passion and felt contented, satisfied. He had confronted his fears and somehow that had left him feeling more grown-up; more sure of himself. His needs were no longer dependent on the approval of others. Dwayne held that thought.

Patter, patter – the soft raindrops fell against the window pane as Dwayne looked out on to the playground. It was nearly spring now and with it came the promise of new growth. This was how fate was talking to Dwayne – or so he felt. He had felt a new relationship emerging between him and the kids; no longer was the air filled with hostility and confrontation. Mutual understanding and respect had crept in. A smile graced his lips as he saw Jenny and Tina approach. He opened the window.

"Hi!" he called.

"Sir, can we come and tidy your class, it's horrible out here." Tina smiled as she said this.

"Please do," came the quick response, "I'm glad you asked."

As he pulled the window shut, he thought of Viv. Would they be lovers? Was his world finally opening up?

"It's been a good day," pondered Dwayne, as he sat in his room nursing a large slice of carrot cake filled with butter cream. The day's events continued to unravel in his mind, right up to the point that he rescued the cellophane wrapped cake from Sainsbury's food shelves. Now that love and friends were in short supply it was his sweet tooth that offered the comfort. Tonight he simply played with the sweet sticky mixture, pondering over whether or not to phone Viv. It had been two days now since he had slept with him and he wanted to be with him tonight. He looked over at his alarm clock – it flashed 10.06 on the digital display. Maybe I should call him, Dwayne continued to play with his cake by taking small creamy flecks on to his tongue. Dwayne remembered Viv saying that he would be in touch as he had pressed Dwayne's phone number into his hip pocket. So maybe he should wait for Viv to call him. Dwayne was now uneasy, as he took further stabs at the cake whilst it nestled in the palm of his hand.

"Damn," he said quietly under his breath as his sense of uneasiness grew. He took a large bite out of the soft crumbly slice, still cradled in his hand.

"Mmmmm ... " A few minutes ticked by on the clock. 'What if Viv was trying to play it cool and was actually waiting for him to call?' Dwayne rolled this around in his mind for a while, in unison with the paste that was now covering the inside of his cheeks, saliva easing it's motion. He let the moist mixture slip down his throat as he allowed thoughts of Viv to slip from his mind for the rest of the night. He still had a few sketch books to mark for 9u, but in reality there was no real rush on this. Dwayne wanted to occupy his mind and this was as good a way as any.

"Ahhhh ... " Eyes tightly shut, Dwayne could feel himself failing. He screamed at the top of his voice until his throat was raw. That's all he could do in the split seconds left to him. He opened his eyes suddenly. His bedroom ceiling was vaguely familiar in the darkness. The luminous face of the alarm clock shone 5.36 at him. He glared at it angrily now as though it was responsible for his fretful sleep; as though it was responsible for the nightmare; as though it was responsible for the ghastly feeling inside of him – the feeling that nobody cared. He shut his eyes again but then opened them. Dwayne felt scared now ... sure he was scared of nightmares; but more than that, he was scared of being alone in the world. He stared upward until dawn came.

16

The week had passed and still no word from Viv. Dwayne wasn't sure what to do with the telephone number on the small piece of paper that he was now playing with between his thumb and forefinger. He had called Viv three times now and all the time he got the same message over the phone. "Sorry, no-one's in right now, but please leave a message after the tone." Maybe this time I should, thought Dwayne. Though he did hate talking to machines, he needed to see Viv again; now that he had tasted the cherry he needed more. But the nagging thought that all that was between him and Viv was sex kept the now screwed up telephone number a moment longer between his fingers. Why hadn't Viv called him? The turmoil continued in his head as he crossed the busy Brixton High Road to a call box. He fumbled around for a ten pence in his pocket, found one, then dropped it in the box. The now familiar answerphone picked up his call.

"Please leave a message after the tone," it instructed. "Blee...eep."

"Hi Viv, this is Dwayne. Just calling to say hi and to ask you if you'd like to meet up sometime this coming week. Give me a call ... okay."

Viv pulled deeply on his cigarette as he heard the message coming through his answerphone. The whirring sound from the tape ground slowly as every syllable was stored.

"Who's Dwayne?" asked Chris casually, lying beside him and stroking his hair.

After another week of silence, Dwayne realised that both he and Viv were history – just a one night fling. It was as though a switch had tripped in his head. Dwayne stopped what he was doing and leaned his elbows on the edge of his desk so as to raise his hands to his face. A study light illuminated the work he had been marking. His whole body began to shudder as a sudden rage rose within him, a fierce uncontrollable rage; a rage that Dwayne had been frightened to acknowledge; a rage that had been born out of his pain. He slammed his hands down on to his desk. Bang! BANG! BANG! BANG! He couldn't stop. BANG!! went his fists as he pummelled the desk top, harder and harder. Splinters flew as the desk lamp smashed against the edge of the desk on it's descent to the floor. Dwayne paused to glare at the tiny reflective shards that were like his life scattered over the floor. He didn't care, he was tired of caring. He pounded the desk once more. BANG!! He stopped now as a calm washed over him, he was back in control. His body had stopped shaking but was now slumped over the desk, exhausted. He gasped for air. Thin shallow intakes that went on into the night long after Dwayne had cleared up the splinters; long after he had brushed his teeth, washed his face and changed for bed; long after he had acknowledged that it had been blatantly obvious that he and Viv had never been destined for anything long term; long after he admitted that he had just chosen to ignore the fact; and long after he had laid down to welcome sleep to his tired body.

With only two days of teaching practice left, Dwayne felt relatively good. He was looking forward to being able to let his hair down, figuratively speaking. To put the hard times behind him. Painting the town red was top of his agenda. Perhaps I'll visit The Village again, thought Dwayne, as he entered the last grade in his mark book. He looked up at the staffroom clock and realised that his free period was up. The bell would ring in the next few minutes. Swiftly collecting up his things, he made for the door as it swung open.
"Oh, hi Kate," he said as he recognised the heavy set eyes and snub nose of his colleague.
"Ahh ... Hiya. It's quiet in here today," she continued. "Where is everyone?"
"I'm not sure," Dwayne shifted his eyes, "perhaps preparing for next half-term's exams."
Kate raised her eyebrows, "Oh yeah ... good thing we don't have to be here for those." A smirk spread across her face. "Hey ..." Her sentence was interrupted by the ringing of the bell. "I was just going to say," she smiled," that it would be nice to celebrate the end of TP by having a drink together. The pub down the road looks good or maybe that small coffee shop ... "
"Yeah, sounds good," said Dwayne hurriedly, "I'll speak to you later." He brushed passed her into the corridor. Kate watched his slim figure disappear down the hallway, books in hand and wondered at his dress sense. The loud mustard-coloured wool jacket did not

blend into her (or the school's – for that matter) more conservative tastes. She sat down carefully in one of the easy chairs arranged around the room, taking care not to crease her navy blue plaid skirt as she did so. There was something about Dwayne that she found intriguing but she couldn't really put her finger on what it was. There was an openness that she liked but at the same time a reserve – like a guard or shield that came down if one got too close. She mulled these thoughts over in her head and felt that perhaps it would be nice to get to know Dwayne better. She looked forward now with more vigour to their coffee date, the day after next.

A feeling of relief swept over Dwayne as he closed his register for the last time at this school. This relief was tinged with sadness as he would genuinely miss the kids that he had taught, even those that had given him grief; the staff with their breezy conversation; and the bricks and mortar of the place. He smiled wearily to himself. He thought about the way in which some of the kids had cheered when he had announced his departure, knowing full well that they were sorry to see him leave. They were afraid to show their feelings as he had once been. A few had said, "Ahhhhh sir, why are you leaving?"

Some had simply said, "Ahhhhhhhh ... " Dwayne snapped the fasteners of his case into place now as he made that final walk down the corridor to the staffroom. Dwayne wondered how Kate had faired.

In Bella's coffee shop, Kate offered to buy the first round of coffee and cake. There was a generous side to Kate's nature that was immediately warming and telling. Dwayne wondered at the love and sharing that had given rise to her kind easy manner. He wondered why he hadn't taken more notice of her before now.

"There you go," said Kate kindly, placing the Black Forest Gateau with extra cream in front of Dwayne, and the Chocolate Fudge Cake opposite for herself. She sat down carefully in the brown and cream suit that now flattered her full form. "Well cheers," she said raising a coffee cup off the tray next to her. "Here's to luck in finding a job."

"Cheers!" Dwayne smiled back.

Kate looked Dwayne square in the eyes. "So, tell me about yourself, Dwayne." Her eyes were warm and shimmering.

"Well," said Dwayne hesitantly, "where does one start?" He wasn't sure which path this question was supposed to lead him down.

"Well, start by telling me about your family," she offered.

The time moved on – five o'clock became six o'clock and then six o'clock became seven, as they both cheerfully exchanged family stories involving various incidents and bust-ups over the Christmas turkey. Kate laughed freely, rocking her head back and forth. She in turn made Dwayne feel free; free and open. He felt himself warming to Kate that bit more. Kate in turn felt that she could move closer to Dwayne having discovered that like her, he too had suffered much parental pressure whilst growing up. For Dwayne much of this had revolved around schooling, career prospects, and marriage, whilst for Kate it revolved strictly around her finding a suitable spouse, preferably before her biological clock stopped ticking. Her pale olive skin glistened now under the bright lights that were Bella's.

She looked down at her wrist watch, "Crumbs! Ten past seven. Dwayne, I've got to fly."

"Okay," said Dwayne, "I've enjoyed our drink, let's meet up again soon – yeh?"

"Let's," Kate smiled. They both rose and walked out of the cafe, making their way back to the tube line.

That night Dwayne slept soundly.

17

Saturday night came and Dwayne was in buoyant spirits. He was looking forward to a night on the town and perhaps, if he got lucky, a boyfriend. He smiled to himself in the mirror, fastened his black bomber jacket, then made his way down to Charing Cross Station. Up the steps, to the right and he could hear the music oozing out of the sophisticated bar named Kudos. Dwayne felt confident as he made his way through the crowded bar area, surveying the faces that he passed. The European faces that stared back at him all looked attractive to him. Dwayne felt that perhaps this had more to do with his new-found freedom than with anything else. Rather like a starving man being offered a feast – everything looks fantastic. As Dwayne placed his order for a K cider he noticed someone to the side of him, staring directly at him. He glanced sideways to get a better look. The young man's eyes narrowed as he did so. Everything that needed to be said was in that look – yes you, I fancy you. Dwayne smiled meekly. The young man's thin lips smiled back at him. What now? thought Dwayne, not quite sure of himself.

"That will be two pounds please," said the attractive Italian-looking barman. Dwayne switched his attention to purchasing his drink.

"Thanks," he said, as he handed over the two gold coins. As he slid the bottle towards his side of the bar a hand tapped him lightly on the right shoulder. It was the young English guy that had smiled at him earlier. Soft curls framed his face.

"Hi, my name's Tony. What's yours?"

"Dwayne," he said, turning to face him squarely.

"I haven't seen you in here before," continued the young man, sweeping the curls from his forehead. "Is this your first time here?"

"No," said Dwayne rather vaguely, not wanting to appear too green. "So where do you usually hang out then, when you're not here?" asked Dwayne swiftly, wanting to keep the conversation going. He liked this guy already. He found his rather classic bone structure particularly attractive though he wasn't sure about the lips.

"Well, shall we say that I don't really have a regular hang out, but I like it in The Village and the Yard ..."

"Ah ... right," responded Dwayne, as they edged closer to each other; both wanting to dispense with the small talk but having to go through the protocol. Conversation began to drag. Half an hour later Tony invited Dwayne back to his place. With his light blue jeans straining at the crutch, Dwayne eagerly took up the invite.

An hour later, having trekked across London by tube, they arrived at Tony's small bedsit, somewhere in Archway. Dwayne wasn't sure of the street – he didn't care for such details anyway. Once inside Tony said nothing, but simply busied himself with the task of seeking out some coffee. This was kind of strange, thought Dwayne, as no question as to whether he wanted coffee or not had been asked. The untidy sitting area and unmade bed came as an even greater surprise to Dwayne. It didn't seem to go with Tony's carefully shaven chin and neatly clad body. The subtle whiff of Obsession did not indicate a slob in his book. He turned around, inquisitively eyeing every space for further clues to Tony's character. His fastidious sensibilities were further assaulted by the sight of what looked like grease stains up the wall against which rested a small Bell cooker. Dwayne tried to console himself with the thought that perhaps he had misjudged the situation and the bedsit would normally have been neater than this. Quickly he disregarded the state of the room as Tony turned around cradling two full mugs of coffee. Dwayne tried not to scrutinise the state of the mug as he drunk from it lest there should be any other uninviting surprises. A mutual smile passed their lips as the last dregs of the bitter sweet beverage were slurped down. Tony's slim fingers were guiding as they both moved over to the bed.

Once undressed their slim bodies moved easily together. Dwayne lay back and let out a low groan as the pleasure surged through him. Cum shot out as they continued to move in frenzied unison.

"Your turn," Tony smiled at Dwayne dreamily.

Sunday didn't come for what seemed an eternity to Dwayne. When he awoke Tony was looking at him in a tender manner.

"Hi," he said quietly.

"Hi," said Dwayne, wiping the sleep from his eyes. Warm air wafted from Tony's nostrils into Dwayne's face, it felt wonderful.

Tony nuzzled Dwayne's right cheek as he let his thoughts wonder. He liked Dwayne, he liked him a lot. Outside of his steady partner Ben, Dwayne was the most considerate man he had met in a long while ... it was a shame really to have to let him go. He knew that he only had room for one lover in his life and having fuck buddies never did work for Tony, feelings always got in the way – no, definitely not for him. He sighed and drew his head back so that he could look at Dwayne's sweet face, relaxed and content.

"Dwayne, we need to talk, man."

Dwayne hadn't bothered to ask Tony about partners – last night he hadn't wanted to know – he had only been interested in immediate gratification; but now he knew the score. He was beginning to learn the rules of the game, but he wasn't sure that he wanted to be a player anymore. He went home feeling a little less loved and a little less cared for than the night before.

As Dwayne surveyed the faces in the seats on either side of him, he was feeling glad to be heading home, back to Cambridge. At least there his love had a place, though not always comfortable he knew he was cared for. The countryside sped past the window in a blur as the train took him on to his destination. Opposite him sat a rather sporty young woman, with long, straight brown hair and weather-hewn features. Her eyelids flickered over light brown eyes that looked interesting and friendly. Her gaze met his as they both stared out of the window. She smiled weakly; Dwayne's lips responded by rising gently. She then returned her gaze to a copy of *Elle* splayed out in her lap.

"Morning! Tickets please," came the bright breezy voice of the ticket inspector. A large, shapely, black woman appeared from behind him, hand outstretched. Her neat wine-coloured jacket matched her neatly pressed hairstyle which rested on her shoulders. The shine on her hair matched the shine on her large full lips. Dwayne slipped his fingers into his right hand jacket pocket and pulled out his ticket. "Thank you," she said in the same chirpy manner.

"Thanks," said Dwayne, replacing the stamped ticket. As she passed down the aisle, Dwayne wondered what sort of family she had, what kind of friends. He imagined she had a lot of friends with a temperament like hers. He leaned back into his seat, arching the back of his neck toward the head rest. His eyelids shut slowly as he relaxed. He thought back to his night at Kudos and his meeting with Tony. His neck arched further. The low lights of Kudos entered his mind again, along with it's cruisy atmosphere. He couldn't help but wonder why he hadn't seen any black guys that night. Maybe he had to look elsewhere for his own skin colour. After all why should the gay sub-culture be any different to the wider, more dominant, heterosexual culture. Was he being naive to think that the gulf between black and white would simply evaporate because of a person's sexual leanings? Dwayne lingered on this for a few moments before allowing other thoughts to catch up with him. His mad dash for the train surged to the fore. The tense moments as the ticket clerk took his money and leisurely punchied out his ticket details.

His day-dreaming was interrupted by the girl in front tapping him lightly on the arm.

"Sorry to disturb you," she whispered in a low voice, "but have you got the time."

"Uhhh ... ten past twelve," he replied dreamily.

"Oh, right thanks," she said now biting her lower lip ever so subtly, "I was reading in this magazine that today I would meet someone special, "she continued in her low tone, "and I think that you might be the person."

"What?" sputtered Dwayne. "Are you winding me up?" He smiled as he said this, suspecting that he was now the butt of some joke.

"No," she said leaning forward. "It say's right here." She pointed to the page in front of her, then leaned further forward and gazed wickedly into his eyes. Dwayne felt a surge of excitement coursing up from his stomach. He sure wasn't used to this happening on his usual journey back home.

"Refreshments sir?"

His eyes opened. The bright light from the window momentarily blinded him.

"Ummmm ... no thanks," he replied nonchalantly.

"Ummmm-wa," went Hyacinth's lips, as she kissed her son on the cheek. Dwayne handed over the bunch of yellow and lilac flowers that he had bought from the market.

"For you Mum." He beamed as she ushered him inside. "So how are things, Mum? You look well."

"Oh fine," she said, whilst resting her flowers down on the kitchen counter. Dwayne slipped off his jacket, then proceeded to search for a vase whilst his mum unwrapped the blooms. "So," Hyacinth continued; now with her back toward Dwayne, "how's the big smoke then? Buoy they must be working you hard – you look thin." Dwayne didn't respond to that, 'usual thing' he thought.

"Where's Quisha and Wes then, have they gone out or something?"

"No, I think Wesley's finishing off some article or another, locked away in that room of his, and Quisha's getting ready for her evening class tonight."

"Oh yes, aromatherapy, right? Is that what's making the house smell so sweet, Mum?" chided Dwayne. "Or is it that you're treating yourself to a new perfume."

Hyacinth turned her neck round and smiled, "If only."

Dwayne handed his mum a suitable receptacle for the flowers just in time for her to transfer their dripping stems without marking her shining work counter. There was a pause in the conversation whilst Hyacinth turned her full attention to the business of arranging and sprucing her gift.

"Listen, I'll go put these bags down in my room ... say hi to the others ... then fill you in on how my teaching prac went."

"Okay," said Hyacinth merrily, with her head half turned over her shoulder.

Quisha was bent over a box of oils when Dwayne glanced into her room.

"Hiya, Quish – how's my favourite sis doing then?"

She looked up and smiled, then got up and gave her brother a hug. "It's been a while," she said.

"I know," said Dwayne. She was glad to see him looking more cheerful; more like his old self. He still looked tired around the eyes but without the dogged weariness he'd had over the Christmas holidays. "Hey come check out these oils, Dwayne, you'll love them. I've got lavender, sandalwood, myrrh." She fingered the small bottles carefully as she held each one up for Dwayne to admire. Wesley's door opened at that moment.

"Oh God! Has Quisha got those oils out again?" said Wesley wryly, eyebrows raised to the sky. His younger brother laughed.

"Are you not getting into it then, Wes?" laughed Dwayne.

"Getting into it?" he chortled. "Not on your life. I'm sticking to body sprays and the usual chemical crap, at least I know where I am with those." They all laughed. It was good to be home.

Later on in the evening he told Quisha about his fling with Tony – he needed to talk to someone about it. She listened quietly and then said, "Just be careful, won't you Dwayne?" That was her only comment before moving on to talk about the love of her life. Quisha was glad that her brother could confide in her, but a nagging part of her couldn't help worrying that her little brother was heading for a fall. His new relish for promiscuity seemed to be the tonic he needed but she wondered how long that would last.

6389 were the final digits Dwayne tapped out on the phone pad. It seemed strange not to be calling Lisa or Pete on his return home, but they were in the past now and Kate was in the present.

"Hello," came her bubbly voice.

"Hi," said Dwayne, "just calling to find out how you're enjoying the half-term break. Started any job applications yet?"

"You're joking aren't you?" she chuckled. Dwayne knew she prided herself on being efficient and had probably sent off at least two applications since the morning. "I've got to start on that tomorrow," she continued. "I've just finished typing up the final assignment, reflecting on TP."

"But that doesn't have to be done till we get back to college," said Dwayne, raising his voice slightly. She was making him feel guilty now for not using this break for work.

"Hey, let's not talk about work," Kate said soothingly. Tell me about your plans for the rest of the week. Are you going to see any movies?" They chatted casually for another ten minutes before Dwayne hung up. He was getting to like Kate a lot and they had arranged to go for a coffee when he got back to London.

18

A week later Dwayne stood by the large branch of Top Man just by Oxford Circus tube station, waiting for his friend Kate. Being a few minutes early, Dwayne surveyed the sea of faces passing both in and by the superstore. He loved the rich variety that he saw before him, that was London. On the dot of one o' clock Kate's smiling face appeared as she ascended the subway steps.

"Hi! Bang on time, eh?" Kate was panting slightly as the words were slung out.

"Of course," smirked Dwayne.

"Can I quickly nip down to Debenhams to check out a perfume for my mum's birthday?" she asked. "It won't take long anyway, I know exactly what she wants."

"What's that then?" asked Dwayne as they moved off in the direction of Bond Street.

"Oh, some Chanel Number Four – it's beautiful."

"Mmmm ..... good taste, your mum." Dwayne turned his head sideways to smile as they continued to navigate their way along the frenzied West End street. When finally at the main entrance to Debenhams, Dwayne held the door open for Kate to pass through. Instead a rather hassled-looking male shopper jostled in front of Kate and sped toward the escalators – mid-afternoon was always a bad time to be in this part of town. Kate and Dwayne looked at each other in a knowing way, then negotiated their own way through the doors. A bored voice over the intercom said, "Ladies and gentlemen, please can I draw your attention to our special promotion for today on Elizabeth Arden's new perfume ... " Dwayne didn't bother to listen to the rest as he eyed a cute-looking guy with pretty eyes coming down from the upper floor via the escalator. Dwayne wondered why it was that men were attracting his eye more than women of late but then let it go. Kate interrupted his thoughts.

"Have a smell of this, Dwayne," she held her wrist to his nose. The scent was pure sensuality. He could appreciate the price tag. They left the store a few moments later with Kate lighter in cash but feeling wealthier for caring. Again this reinforced Dwayne's feelings for Kate and drew them just that little bit closer.

In the Dome coffee bar, not far from their original meeting place, Dwayne bought the first round of coffee but this time they both agreed to leave the cream cakes alone.

"So tell me about your love life Dwayne ... any relationships on the go right now?" Kate was grinning suspiciously as she spooned frothy cappuccino into her mouth. Her no-beating-about-the-bush straight-out-with-it approach was now becoming more evident to Dwayne. "Anyone special in your life?" she reiterated, seeing that she had caught Dwayne somewhat unawares.

"I wish," said Dwayne wistfully, staring into the dark brown liquid that was now steaming under his nose. Kate sucked the froth from her spoon noisily as she surveyed the dark black lashes that were now obscuring the eyes beneath them; the eyes that she wanted to read and indeed enter into in some strange way. Her mind was feeling out the territory that marked her own boundaries, her own thoughts, feelings, and needs. She would tread carefully. She felt a rush of emotion as Dwayne's eyelids slowly raised, his eyes deep and brown peered up at her.

"I reckon that I need to change my aftershave to some of that Chanel Number Four." They both laughed. "My relationships are going well if they last a full night," he jibed. Kate continued to laugh, feeling at ease with Dwayne's sense of humour.

"Ahhhh," she said finally, sweeping her hair away from her face. "I shouldn't be laughing really. It's not as though I've faired any better. Well, what kind of women do you go for?" she probed further.

"Who said I go for women?" said Dwayne slyly. He viewed Kate's face carefully to see a reaction; to sense with every conceivable organ if rejection was on her lips.

"Ohhh ... well ... I can handle that," said Kate, looking slightly off step. Somewhere in the back of her mind she had sensed a possibility rested in Dwayne to be with a man but now she needed to know whether or not the possibility also rested for him to be with a woman. That would help her to determine the scope of their relationship. The strength of feeling that Dwayne caused within her was still just that; Kate was still trying to analyse what exactly it was that she wanted from him.

"Look," said Dwayne hesitantly "I might as well tell you straight out ... I go for both women and men ... get it?"

Kate's brow furrowed.

"Crumbs, that's complicated," she offered, having regained her step.

"Tell me about it," remarked Dwayne dryly. "My family still think it's a phase I'm going through."

Kate nodded in sympathy, not that she really understood Dwayne's dilemma but she knew what families could be like.

Dwayne continued, "I think that my Mum would be happier if I was totally gay rather than in the middle you know? One or the other for her." He felt the old feelings of hurt creeping back and checked himself. He could feel tears welling up at the back of his eyes – Kate noticed this and looked away, sensing Dwayne's awkwardness.

After a few seconds silence Kate returned her gaze to Dwayne's face.

"It's always easier for people to pigeonhole each other." Her manner was emollient and soothing. Life had taught her not to judge others and, equally importantly, how to empathise. Their eyes smiled at each other as an air of easiness permeated the space between them.

"I've got to get a cream cake," said Dwayne after a few minutes. "How about you?"

Kate nodded.

Though life for Dwayne now seemed less stressful, his energy seemed to be slowly seeping away from him. He pined for a lover; his mind needed distraction. Work provided that but his body and soul were left wanting. He sought a new fix – chocolate and cream cakes were the obvious choice. At least he wasn't going down the path of drugs and booze or so he reasoned. Night after night the compulsion grew.

Two weeks on, Kate was bouncing up the steps leading to Dwayne's college digs. She had a spring in her step and a smile on her lips. She was feeling good and didn't mind showing it. This was the first time that she would be visiting Dwayne on his own turf. His room would give her fresh insight into the man that was increasingly filling her thoughts. Dwayne inhaled deeply as he heard the gentle tapping on his room door.

"Hi Kate!" He ushered Kate into his room, gently guiding her body by the elbow. His touch conveyed intimacy; her body yielded, taking up the offer of the armchair in the corner of the room. Her eyes scanned the room momentarily whilst Dwayne settled on the side of his bed. She eyed the neatly made bed; the smooth shiny surface of the sink over in the opposite corner of the room; the buffed surface of the mirror above it; all required attention. Her eyes rested on the family-size box of eclairs sitting on his desk.

"Honestly Dwayne, we're going to have to call you Mr Creamy," she chuckled, "and I'm not talking about your pants." They both exploded into a fit of laughter. However, Dwayne's laughter became stifled as it dawned on him that this was no longer a laughing matter. He reached over, offering Kate one of the eclairs straight from the box. He swallowed his with urgency, negating the need for niceties such as a plate or napkins. Kate mouthed her cake delicately, not wanting to smudge the fresh cream over her satin lipstick. The cream in Dwayne's stomach was simply laying undigested along with the soured remains of the last two cakes he had swallowed before Kate's arrival. He eyed the last cake as it lay in it's box taunting him. What the hell, he thought to himself as he reached over to pick it up. Kate contentedly swallowed the last of her eclair, then dabbed her lips with a small tissue from the pocket at the front of her Levi jeans. She tossed her head backwards and beamed at Dwayne.

"Mmmmm ... not bad ... not bad at all." Dwayne swallowed hard before nodding in agreement.

"Well, just two more weeks of college and then *finito!*" Kate reminded Dwayne as she left his room that evening, "hang in there!" she said cheerily pecking Dwayne on the cheek. Her manner was casual but the kiss lingered on Dwayne's cheek and her words hung in the air long after she had left the room. As cream curdled in his stomach, Dwayne sat down at his desk to finish his last assignment. However, concentration eluded him as his restless mind conspired with his stomach to make the remains of the evening as uncomfortable for Dwayne as possible. Finally he gave up on what remained of the night and hit the pillow; as he drifted off he made a mental note to stock up on more cake.

19

Although the last assignment was finally out of the way, life was becoming increasingly arduous for our man Dwayne. He was now unable to pinpoint his feelings or where they came from. He only knew that he felt out of sorts. Lethargy and angst had crept up on him in such a quiet fashion that they now went unrecognised. Dwayne increased his consumption of cream and chocolate and hoped for the best. He was looking forward to going to Kudos again at the weekend but this became unrealistic as illness pulled Dwayne down. Disease had taken hold.

Saturday night he stared into his mirror and saw the spots which covered his forehead; he stuck out his tongue and saw the thick white coating; the glands around his neck felt sore. He retreated to his bed. Kate's words came back into his head.

"Rest is all you need Dwayne ... rest."

Perhaps she was right, he would rest tonight and go out Monday night. He reached for a box of comfort which said gateau slices and ate. As he ate his mind said more, more. He ignored the voice in his stomach that was saying stop, no more Dwayne ... no more. He didn't realise that cream from the past few days now lay putrefied in his intestines – clogging up a system that could no longer cope. Just as Dwayne could no longer cope with the weight of his loneliness. The toxins produced were now seeping into his glands and muscles, weighing him down. Just as a depression pressed against his forehead, almost unrelenting to the point where Dwayne no longer felt it. As he continued to ignore his inner voice, the toxins erupted through his skin as spots, but still Dwayne took no notice. He continued to eat.

By Sunday morning Dwayne felt like shit, he thought perhaps he had some kind of flu bug and would have to buy some juice. He had been sick in the night, congealed cream rising from his stomach, now he had lost all desire for food. His body had gained respite for the time being. Now he pulled himself from his bed and dragged himself down the hall in his blue and white pyjamas - putting on his dressing gown was out of the question - into the toilet. He pulled out his dick for a pee. There was a white spot on it. Dwayne gasped ... all sorts of horrible thoughts blazed through his mind. But the one that stuck was that Tony, sweet-looking Tony had given him some horrible disease. But he had been careful, both of them had ... but obviously not careful enough, thought Dwayne, not fucking well careful enough. He finished his pee and went back to bed. The juice would have to wait now until he went to the sex clinic on Monday.

"We'll carry out some routine tests Mr Stevenson, but these look like ordinary spots to me and yes they can occur on a man's penis. From what you've been telling me, you've been run down lately anyhow. Lots of fruit juice and lots of rest is what I would recommend." The doctor's officious manner made Dwayne feel foolish but his words brought waves of relief. His worldly eyes seemed to look him up and down and say, "Don't come in here and waste my precious time please. I didn't spend years at medical school to have some joker like you come in here and waste my time." Dwayne allowed copious amounts of blood to be drained from his arm before sloping off sheepishly through the clinic door.

A week of rest and the odd glass of juice had Dwayne feeling rather better. He felt grateful that at least he was able to join in with the general mood of excitement as the year had finally come to an end. Kate hugged him warmly that day, that warm sunny day and said,
"We did it Dwayne ... we did it." Dwayne hugged her back and it felt good. Really good.

That night Kudos beckoned and Dwayne felt sweet. A generous application of deodorant made him smell sweet too. As he made his way toward Charing Cross Station by tube, his thoughts were a mixture of Kate, school and freedom. He wasn't sure exactly why but he felt an almost giddy sensation – as though he was now floating. In half an hour he had alighted, exited the station barriers and was walking up the steps that would take him back into the busy throng that was London's West End. Already he could hear the voices and music emanating from the busy bar; welcoming sounds to his ears. He entered with the confidence of a regular and scanned the faces carefully now, taking his time. He wondered if he would score again tonight. His tight black 'Destroy' T-shirt with matching black Levi's had already caught the attention of several guys cruising the bar area.

One of them was black, tall and beautiful. Dwayne eyed him back, then stopping a few steps in front of him turned to the bar. He wanted to play this cool; not so eager this time, suss him out a little. Ordering a Perrier water with lemon, Dwayne sipped slowly and waited. Five minutes later he turned around to rekindle the flame in the black Adonis' eyes. Too late. Some other individual seemed to be now kindling with him very nicely; they laughed a shared laugh. Damn, thought Dwayne, feeling somehow slighted, if not a little jealous. The night wore on ...

After two attempts at conversation and his earlier aborted effort, Dwayne was now feeling rather dejected. It was nearly eleven and he didn't want to leave, to go back to an empty room with only the four walls for company. In a paper he picked up from the bar he saw a club called the Vox listed which played his kind of music and promised plenty of action. His mind toyed with the idea of checking it out but before he had made a decision, a rather firm hand touched his left arm.

"Excuse me, have you finished with that?" Dwayne looked into the eyes of the young man, in a puzzled manner. He wasn't sure if he meant the drink or the paper. As if reading his thoughts he said, "*Boyz* - the paper."

"Ahh yes ... help yourself." Dwayne smiled a friendly smile.

"Thanks," came the simple reply. "Anything worth reading this week?" the stranger continued after a pause, flicking through the paper aimlessly.

"Ummm ... sure," responded Dwayne, "I spotted an article on body piercing, but it was only a glance .... kinda looked interesting though, you know." The stranger nodded. Dim lights and loud chatter did not make for easy reading. Dwayne now eyed his new companion more closely as it dawned on him that he was being cruised and that the paper had simply been a prop. He viewed the sultry eyes and closely spaced teeth as the guy stood before him, waiting for the penny to drop, for the switch to trip. Dwayne scanned the rumpled hair and gaunt features that said a lot but gave away nothing. Alarm bells started ringing – he ignored them; his body was lonely and wanting. Nothing short of a ten ton truck would have made an impact on him at that moment. Not until he had gone back to the guy's flat; taken in the reek of stale sweat; sipped the hurriedly-made coffee; surveyed the hurriedly-made bed. Not until he had begun to undress this new stranger; to feel teeth gnawing at his nipples did Dwayne hear the bells. He had been in this loveless situation once too often.

"Stop! Stop!" he cried forcefully now. The stranger's face contorted as he looked up from his quarry.

"What's wrong?" he blurted. Dwayne didn't answer as he hastily pulled himself away. He was now desperate to get out. It felt to Dwayne as though he was suffocating within a clammy case of mud; he was now fighting for air. Dwayne fought with all his might, as if his life now depended on it. Every move he made to the front door was a sweep of gunk from his nostrils. Every step became a gasp for air. He needed love as much as he needed oxygen – one can only hold their breath for so long. As the door slammed shut behind him, Dwayne knew that he had made the right decision. He felt that a shift had taken place in his way of being and that once again another chapter in his life was about to unfold.

PART III

20

The sweet melodic tones of the saxophone, wrapped around Dwayne as he lay quite motionless on his bed. Only the gentle rise and fall of his chest could be perceived in the dimly lit room that he now occupied. He allowed the relaxing, almost ethereal sounds of the album, *Breathless*, to take him away to a world where all was well; where he had no cares, no worries, no fears; a world we all need to escape to from time to time.

'It's weird being back at home again,'

Dwayne mused over in his mind as he looked up at the familiar but strange lampshade that hung from his bedroom ceiling. It's pale-blue paper obscuring the bare light bulb underneath, it's spherical shape encasing an otherwise garish illumination. He closed his eyes and hummed along to the sassy, soothing notes emanating from his small cassette player. A sigh escaped from his open mouth as he allowed himself to be swallowed up by the soft, almost teasing sensation of escape. Nothing was going to bring him back now. This first night back at home was to Dwayne his most blissful for a long while: no marking to do; no screaming kids to think of; and thankfully no more curriculum tick sheets for at least another two months – depending on whether or not he could find a job that is. The creases on Dwayne's forehead were completely erased now as sleep took him.

"Morning sleepy head." Quisha poked her head around the bedroom door and smiled at her kid brother.

"Mmmm ... what time is it?" asked Dwayne, all bleary-eyed and groggy.

"Eleven thirty," said his sister quietly, the smile still on her face. "There's a Kate on the phone for you. What do you want me to tell her? Call back or to hang on?"

"Ummm ... yeah ... ask her to hang on, will you, Sis? Thanks." Dwayne heard the dull thud-thud of Quisha's feet as she padded down the stairs in her open-toed sandals. A warm summer breeze caught the hem of his bedroom curtains, causing them to billow up. Momentarily bright sunshine beamed into his naked face, willing him to get up. He yawned loudly, then in a swift movement pulled away the deep blue bed covers, swung his legs on to the floor, and then launched himself clear of the bed. Without pulling on slippers or sandals he rushed downstairs in bare feet, allowing the coarse texture of the tan carpet to rasp against his skin. He wiped the remains of sleep from his eyes with the right sleeve of his pinstriped pyjamas. Quisha looked up from the *Ebony* magazine resting in her lap, as her slim dark, pencil-like fingers flicked over the next page. Dwayne dropped himself on to the rather sumptuous sofa next to her, then reached over to a small side table on which the phone was resting. Lifting the cool plastic of the receiver to his ear he yawned again.

"Mmmm ... Hiya Kate. How's it going?"

"Pretty good," she replied chirpily. "Good news, I've got a job!" Her voice rose in excitement.

"Wow! That's great!" replied Dwayne enthusiastically. "Really great. I'll have to buck my ideas up now or else I'll be left high and dry, eh?"

"Well ... "

Dwayne interrupted before Kate could get the words out.

"Jees, how many interviews did you say you'd been to before now?"

"Four altogether," remarked Kate calmly.

"Four! I haven't even heard so much as a dicky bird from one of the schools I've applied to."

"You will." Kate's manner was reassuring. "You will."

Dwayne got upbeat. "Anyway, here I am rambling on again ... tell me about the school. Important things first has it got a good canteen?" They both broke into laughter. "Listen," said Dwayne, once the laughter had died down, "why don't we get together to celebrate and you can fill me in when we meet ... yeah?"

"Yeah okay," quipped Kate. "When and where?"

Dwayne hesitated a few seconds before answering. "Ah ... how about ... how about Monday lunch-time? Say one o'clock in Cranks, Leicester Square. You don't mind vegetarian, do you?"

Kate chuckled. "Well let's put it this way, when men ask me whether or not I like meat, I normally tell them I'm strictly vegetarian," her voice went up," but then it depends what kinda meat's on offer." Kate's voice was now infused with innuendo and flirtation.

Dwayne stammered slightly. "Ooo-er ... steady on Kate ... you're not trying to corrupt my young innocent mind, are you?"

Kate chuckled at Dwayne's attempt to diffuse her subtle pass with humour. Almost a side parry in tennis terms. A direct volley is what Kate wanted. She bit her bottom lip involuntarily and said as calmly as possible, "Cranks it is then, one o'clock. Don't be late," she teased.

"Am I ever?" replied Dwayne softly.

"Bye," said Kate.

"Bye."

Kate heard the click as Dwayne replaced the hand set. It was a few seconds before she carefully replaced the ergonomically-shaped plastic to it's resting place in the cradle of the Trimphone. She glared at it's smooth contours and thought of Dwayne; thought of his many contours; thought of how she now knew every groove and hollow on his face; could picture how his hard body would complement her soft one; how she loved his smile, his humour; how she loved his openness, his vulnerability. She sighed now – taking him to the altar in her mind was not necessarily a good idea at this stage. Dwayne had made no suggestion toward changing their relationship. Where they ever destined to be more than friends? This question stayed with her for the rest of the morning, in spite of attempts to dash it.

Back in Cambridge, Dwayne's thoughts were rather different to those Kate had been experiencing. As he sat next to his sister, he was conscious of her flicking pages, almost to a rhythm. He rested his head on the back of the settee whilst digesting the news Kate had given him. A feeling of exhilaration welled up. It was wonderful and he felt pleased for her. In some small way this inspired and prompted him to put even more energy into his own job search. After all, he didn't want to be left behind and jobs would be drying up in a couple of months as June had already begun. Dwayne realised now that he had been a little apathetic in terms of making applications or even reading ads on a regular basis. Dwayne chided himself, time to pull your finger out. He told himself, Jees I don't want to be stuck in Cambridge doing sod all for the rest of the year ... my social life would dry up and I'd probably go gaga. His mind now took off on a tangent – 'Woo, Kate's coming on a bit strong ... she's never flirted with me before ... or maybe I got it wrong, maybe she was just playing with me. Christ, what if she wasn't? What if she really fancies me? What then? Shucks what am I saying, lighten up, why analyse everything?' His thoughts stopped here as he became aware of an elbow in his ribs.

"Kate uh? You're a dark horse, aren't you?" Quisha was beaming at her brother having lost all interest in her magazine. "So come on then, tell big Sis all about her." She patted his right thigh playfully. Just then Hyacinth walked into the room, with a grin on her face.

Woo, saved by the bell, thought Dwayne wistfully. "Morning Mum," he said enthusiastically.

"Morning Dwayne," came the chirpy response. "Still in pyjamas, come on, chop chop, or else it won't be worth getting out of them at all." She smiled a bright smile as she moved toward Quisha. Her oatmeal-coloured, cotton dress moved easily about her body as she did so. "Who's Dwayne been hiding from us Quisha?" Her hand fell on her daughters shoulder. Quisha tittered whilst her brother rolled his eyes.

"Hey look, it's no big deal, Kate's a friend I met at college, that's all." Dwayne made a move to pull himself up from the settee as his mum sat down on the other side of his sister.

"Oh yes, a friend uh?" Hyacinth's voice rose with excitement. "Buoy, it's about time you found yourself a good woman. Is she black?" Lypsyl glistened on her lips as she smiled at her son.

"No, she is not black and no she is not my girlfriend. She's a friend who happens to be female, okay." Dwayne was beginning to feel exasperated – he could sense that he was losing his cool; he had been down this all too familiar path before. His mum deliberately chose to ignore his sexuality by not talking about it or referring to it she was overtly pushing him, almost willing him into any relationship but a homosexual one. Didn't seem to matter who or what kind of woman as long as it was a woman. All of her fears about his future; about her future as a grandmother; or indeed about her notions of normality would be dispelled.

"So tell us about this *friend*," insisted Hyacinth, holding Dwayne from any further advances toward his bedroom.

"Give it a rest will you Mum - for God sake?"

Hyacinth winced, she wasn't expecting this sort of reaction from her son. After all, wasn't it normal for a mother to take an interest in her son's life? Wasn't it normal for a mother to care about her son's happiness ... wasn't it normal? Why was Dwayne behaving like this?

The questions reeled around in Hyacinth's head. The disparity between Hyacinth's requirements for happiness and her son's was glaring but in this heated exchange between mother and son neither could fully appreciate this. Both struggled to meet on common ground; Dwayne in his confusion, Hyacinth in her ignorance. Only Quisha was truly aware of what had taken place; only she was aware of the need for both parties to rise above the old beliefs; to let go of the old expectations.

As Dwayne climbed the stairs he felt overwhelmed with despair. Why was it that his mum still couldn't let him be? Why was it that he still got so angry, so frustrated? Hadn't he moved on now? Hadn't he dealt with his emotions? Reaching the top of the stairs he paused.

"Should I hit the bathroom or the bedroom?" he asked himself. He shuffled back to bed, getting dressed was no longer appealing. Dwayne felt bad as he laid quite rigid under the covers; bad for having shouted at his mum; for having caused her distress; bad for feeling bad. He sank into a fitful slumber as he searched in his dreams for salvation.

21

The smell of wholesome baking and herbal teas meshed together to create the nutty odour that wafted past Dwayne's nose as he leant against the food counter at Cranks. He eyed the colourful array of foods. There were pizza wedges covered with melted cheese and black olives; soya rolls; lentil bake; rolls with various fillings of nuts, grapes, sun-dried tomatoes; there was fruit trifle and apple crumble. His taste buds were on go. There was a gentle tap on his left shoulder.

"Hiya." It was Kate.

"Hiya, Kate." Instinctively they gave each other a peck on the cheek. Kate smelled wonderful. She was wearing something between vanilla and roses.

"Mmmmm ... I'm hungry. How about you?" enquired Dwayne.

"Ravenous," she replied, eyeing him up as though he had put himself on the menu. He smirked, then turned once more to face the counter of food encased behind the glass screen.

"I'm having the pizza, I think." He wasn't sure.

"The rolls look good," asserted Kate.

"Mmmm ... they do, don't they."

"Can I help you?" prompted the young woman behind the counter. They both became aware of the queue that was now backing up behind them. They smiled a knowing smile at one another.

"I'll have the salad roll please," offered Kate.

"Make that two please," pitched in Dwayne – his friend smiled again at him.

"Anything to drink with that?" came the brisk voice.

"Ahh, a dandelion coffee would be good for me. Kate?"

"A regular coffee for me please." The young woman hastily obliged.

"I'll get this," said Dwayne quietly into Kate's left ear, "it's my treat today."

"Ooo ... thanks," crooned Kate.

"You're welcome." Their eyes met briefly before the young lady interrupted.

"That will be four pounds thirty please." The same brisk voice. The cash register bell rang and the amount entered. "There's your change – seventy pence – thank you."

"Thank you," replied Dwayne, as he and Kate moved off to find a free table. There was a two-seater next to the window. The modern iron-backed chairs and polished wooden tables gave the place a Bohemian feel. Dwayne admired a rather abstract-looking painting on the far wall as he gingerly placed his tray down on the table. Kate's eyes followed him for a brief moment before she too placed her tray down on the table.

"Nice, eh?" she offered casually.

"Yeah, kind of," replied Dwayne. "Reminds me of some of my earlier work."

"Oh really," Kate's eyes were alight with interest.

"Well, college days really, when I fancied myself as a cubist." They chuckled together – not so much because of what had been said but because they enjoyed being together – there was a certain something that kept sparkling. The question that remained was would Dwayne allow it to ignite? "Changing the subject – tell me about this job you've landed." Dwayne's voice was insistent.

"Well, it's at Parliament Hill, an all girls school in Camden. It's kind of relaxed you know and I like that." She was interrupted.

"But how do you feel about it being all girls?"

"Oh, that's not a problem – kids are kids, right?"

"Hmm ... sure ... but I like a mix myself." The conversation rambled on for a good thirty minutes as chunks of food were forced down between breaths. How Dwayne loved to watch Kate's chestnut eyes as she spoke – he felt that he knew the next sentence that was coming even before the words came out. What was this warm feeling that had grown between them? Could it be friendship of an intimate kind? Or could it be more? Maybe more importantly, *should* it be more? Dwayne continued to rehearse this thought as he scanned the animated features before him, the features in which he now saw such beauty. He was amused at the way her little snub nose danced with her lips, the way her dark brown hair now played with the skin on her forehead causing her to sweep it away every few minutes.

"Well, I guess we had better make a move, before we take root eh?" A spot of light danced in Dwayne's eyes as he spoke. Kate screwed her lips into a wry smile as she felt a reluctance to leave.

"What time do you have to catch your train?" she asked.

"Mmm ... not until six, I guess but I need to catch the library back in Cambridge before it shuts ... so we've got time."

"Good." Kate paused. "How do you feel about visiting the Tate then? There's a exhibition on there by a German artist who does these amazing things with metal and kinetics. Apparently, she has managed to simulate various functions of the body through the use of perpetual motion and various metals. I think it'll be good." Her eyebrows went up.

"I'm game," said Dwayne enthusiastically, "It'll make a change to look at art outside of a classroom for a change." He chuckled lightly. With that they got up and made for the tube. As they waited on the platform Dwayne observed the fact that this was the first time that he had seen Kate in her casual's. The faded blue denims matched her simple T-shirt. She wore white Reebok trainers without any socks. This in itself spoke volumes to Dwayne, reinforcing in his mind the easiness in which Kate carried herself – she exuded a confidence that belied appearance. The train arrived and they got on. Dwayne instinctively guiding Kate with a hand around her shoulders. They clumped themselves into a seat facing their direction of travel.

"Mind the doors please," commanded a voice over the intercom. Just as the doors were closing on leapt a young man with a backpack. The door slid together swiftly, just missing the young man's head but clamping his backpack in a vice-like grip. His face went red as he struggled to pull free. Kate and Dwayne looked on with strained faces lest they burst out laughing, embarrassing the poor lad further. Seeing the futility of struggling, the young man stopped squirming and simply stood still, looking forlorn, until the doors slid open again. He pulled free quickly and found a seat with equal speed, wrestling free of the offending object. His skin now cleared as he regained some composure. Passengers, including Dwayne and Kate, smiled at him sympathetically. He looked away as the train lurched forward.

Alighting at Pimlico the couple made their way to the Tate, hand in hand. Kate's heart was thumping with joy as their physical contact now solidified her dreams yet further. For Dwayne this contact was instinctive rather than romantic and had served only to confuse his mind further. He was now aware of Kate's new feelings towards him: was he being fair to her? His thoughts about finding a boyfriend were still as strong as ever. Would she be tying him down to a monogamous relationship? What kind of commitment would she want? Did she need? The questions seemed to ricochet within his skull, causing distress rather than comfort. His wind pipe constricted. Wasn't it clear that Kate was offering something that he had needed for a long time? She loved him, didn't she? Or at least cared for him. Did he care for her in the same way though? Was she the one for him? Had they known each other long enough? He thought back to his relationship with Candice ... whilst being with her his need for men had never faded. Did he some how feel guilty about that? Was it guilt and angst that were now keeping him at arms length from Kate? Was it, indeed, he who was creating the web of misery, isolation, and confusion that so pervaded his life? This question had cropped up before but still ... Dwayne struggled now with his breathing as he did with his mind. He paused in mid-stride momentarily but then carried on in silence. Kate clasped his hand tighter. He scolded himself for being afraid to love. For wasn't that the truth? That he was now afraid? The questions stopped as they ascended the steps to the gallery.

Dwayne drew his hand away from Kate's, pretending to search for a tissue. His breathing had now become so shallow that he was taking the air in through his mouth. Kate turned to him looking visibly concerned.

"Are you okay Dwayne – why all the huffing and puffing? You need to do some jogging." She laughed half-heartedly, as she could see no amusement on Dwayne's face.

"Oh ... " Dwayne gasped, "I'm fine, just need to rest for a few minutes on these steps." They both sat down on the cold stone. "Like you said," he continued, "I need to do some exercise – get some stamina back. Anyway, I'm fine now." His breathing had eased. He smiled at Kate weakly. Far from convinced, Kate let it drop.

As they entered the main entrance to the Tate, they couldn't help but take in the grandeur of the interior. The lofty ceilings and ceramic tiled floors stamped upon one the impression of being in some great Roman palace. It takes one back to a time when on the one hand, you had the excesses of an imperial state with it's pillage and arrogance and yet, on the other hand, one is transported to a period of personal freedom – a time when homosexuality wasn't frowned upon. They traipsed behind a group of tourists speaking in Italian, German, and French. As they passed through two huge stone columns they entered into the main hall.

"Wow," gasped Dwayne, "check it out." An immense vascular tangle of iron and steel stretched out before them. Mercury pumped through glass tubing as if taking on a life of it's own. Dwayne couldn't help but smile as he drew parallels between the tangled mass before them and his own life. As soon as he thought he had untangled one knot in his life another appeared. As he looked on he felt all the irksome droplets of his life were collecting around two areas: guilt and insecurity. Like the vision before him, they needed to be pumped from his veins. At times he felt good about being different and about himself; about being able to explore and experience both the heterosexual world and the homosexual; about having experienced a white and a black culture. However, at times he couldn't help but hate himself a little for not fitting in, for not being one thing or the other ... life would be so much easier. But then again, maybe life wasn't meant to be easy. Dwayne's head felt heavy.

"Penny for your thoughts," interrupted Kate.

"Ha, ha," laughed Dwayne, "They'll cost a little more than that."

Kate put a hand to his cheek and kissed him on the lips. Dwayne returned her intensity.

On the journey back home to Cambridge, Dwayne made a mental note not to mention what happened between him and Kate to either Quisha or his mum – not for now at any rate. He was sure that they would only increase the pressure he already felt. As he watched the sun just ducking below the skyline, Dwayne allowed the day's events to speed through his head, just as the scenery now sped before him. His breathing grew deeper as he allowed himself to unwind. Kate infused every pore of his body. He looked forward to their movie date in a week's time. Maybe he would have an interview by then.

22

Back within the familiar surrounds of Cambridge Library, Dwayne was on the second floor, flicking through the latest copy *of The Times Educational Supplement*. He sat at one of the heavy oak-wood tables, next to the rack of quality newspapers.

"Shit ... nothing," he said quietly under his breath as he scanned the pages hungrily. 'Excellent prospects for the right candidate' read one ad 'Co-ed comprehensive. Church of England'. So many were like that and Dwayne had no particular calling to work in a school with a strong religious ethic. He carried on flicking. Just as he reached the last page of ads in the section on art secondary, his eyes caught a general advert splashed on the opposite page. 'Quentin Kinestan, St Johns Wood. We are a co-ed looking to fill several teaching posts. English, Geography, and Art.' He scribbled down the details. This place sounded perfect. It was co-ed, in London and non-religious. Dwayne's spirits rose as he felt hopeful once again. Maybe his prayers would be answered this time. In the last two days he had begun to realise how much was riding on him finding a job. His independence for a start. Anyway, he didn't want to go back to provincial life again. He thought back to the upset with his mum a few days ago. Again the question – why had he got so angry? An elderly lady walked past Dwayne's chair, brushing her handbag against the back of his shoulder blades. Neither parties noticed. Dwayne swam now in search of the answer to his question, diving deeper and deeper. Perhaps like his mum, like Wesley, he needed also to grow and to expand his thinking. Perhaps instead of judging them as they judged him, he needed to attempt to understand them, to understand how they saw life, to allow them the time to dissolve not only the homophobic thinking from their own life time but from the generation before them. Ultimately if he loved himself then he needed to let go of the anger that continued to brew within him. He needed to let go of the old thinking, let go of the pain. If he could manage this then maybe, just maybe they could do the same. Somehow there was clarity in all the confusion that still waged within his head.

Dwayne snapped back to his present surroundings. It was a gorgeous summer's day outside and he had no intention of spending the whole day in a stuffy library. He left by the stairs feeling buoyant and light. His lightweight leather sandals made a slapping sound on the tiled steps as he descended.

For a change Dwayne was glad to be spending time on his own. As he sipped cappuccino from a small ceramic cup in Henry's, there was an air of sublimity in his actions. His concentration was fixed more surely on the people who were passing the window by which he sat than on the hot steaming cup pressed to his lips. He had almost forgotten how much he loved café culture; relaxing and simply people-watching. It was a wonderful luxury simply to let the day ebb by. Sun reflecting off someone's steel watch caused him to squint momentarily. 'I wonder what Kate's doing right now', he thought to himself. 'I wonder what or who she's thinking of'. He took another sip from his cup, making a slight slurping sound as air was sucked in at the same time. Perhaps this is what I need, more time on my own, more time to think, to read, to do what I want to do. How long has it been since I've even picked up my camera, for crying out loud? Maybe this thing with Kate's getting out of hand; maybe I'm just lining myself up for another dive, for more pain. Dwayne's mind dwelt on the fact that he hadn't exactly scored in the love stakes in recent months. Candice kept cropping up like a hazard light in a thick, but distant mist. A small Asian lady in her mid-fifties smiled at Dwayne as she noticed him gazing out of the window. Instinctively he smiled back. What was this effect of sun on people? Dwayne's mind drifted back to his photography. His art needed expression outside school, outside the classroom. He made a mental note to carry his camera with him on Saturday when he would be meeting up with Kate. He smirked visibly as it dawned on him that he was beginning to organise his life around Kate.

"Jesus – why is life such a tug of war?" Dwayne mumbled the words to himself quietly as he pushed his chair from under him. The question hung in the air as Dwayne paid the bill and made his exit on to the brick-paved courtyard in front of Henry's, joining the hurly burly.

Before making his way home, Dwayne stopped for a pee at the Lion Yard public toilets. At least they're decent was the subconscious choice he had made between these and the one's further on at Drummer Street. He glanced at his image in the mirror as he entered the darkened interior. His new image of short cropped hair was now more in line with his attempts to simplify his life. He registered for a moment the confusion that lurked in his eyes, then turned to make for the urinals. They were crowded. A vacant toilet cubicle saved his bladder from further discomfort. As he allowed the stream of liquid to flow from his body he glanced up at the graffiti that was scrawled almost illegibly on the dark walls. A swastika stood out from the scribble that now invaded Dwayne's senses. He could make out the words, WOGS OUT – THERE IS NO BLACK IN THE UNION JACK. Next to it was an arrow pointing to another sentence, WHICH FASCIST QUEER BASTARD WROTE THIS? read the writing. Dwayne finished his business and flushed the toilet. He no longer felt alarmed by such words when he saw them but perhaps just a little sad. He washed his hands methodically in the sink whilst checking his appearance once more. 'A fitting place for shit is in a toilet,' thought Dwayne dryly to himself, as he now washed all traces of disdain from his mind. He blew his hands under the dryer.

23

"Hi," said Quisha casually as Dwayne entered the hallway, pushing the front door shut behind him.

"Hi, how's it going?" He slipped his door key back into his jeans pocket.

"Fine, how's it going with you?" Quisha moved toward the kitchen, making slapping noises on the cold tiles as she entered. Just behind, Dwayne answered, "Pretty good really. I've spent most of today drinking coffee and people-watching." He smiled whilst perching on the breakfast counter, then continued, "I'm not as cultured about it as you though." Quisha turned from the sink from which she had filled a glass with water; she laughed.

"Oi, watch it, cheeky." Her brother playfully pushed her shoulder. He knew that Quisha loved café culture as much as he did. "Careful." She sipped gingerly from the glass of slopping water.

"How did that poem go?" continued Dwayne. His sister's writing talents often spilt over from her job.

"One sec, let me think." Quisha lifted her eyes to the ceiling, then set her glass down awkwardly on the breakfast bench next to her brother's elbow. She herself then sat down on a wooden stool immediately under the bench. Dwayne breathed impatiently. "Oh I've got it." Quisha uttered the first few lines as they came to her:

> Sitting, idly watching from a coffee shop window as people;
> Rush, idle, amble, cruise, saunter.
> In between sips of coffee, one can take a moment to gaze at the world outside;
> Frenzied, busy, whizzing, crazy, ecstatic.

"Can't remember the rest."

She pulled her lips into a blank expression, then took another sip of water.

"Well, that's cool anyway," Dwayne paused, "you certainly have a gift there, Sis." He smiled before changing the direction of conversation. "So where's Mum?"

"Mmmm ... " This was all Quisha could manage whilst draining the contents of her glass. "She nipped out to the shops ... to get those current buns Wes loves so much." Dwayne looked surprised. "Yes, I meant to tell you," his sister continued, "he rang earlier on. He's coming home this Saturday."

"Oh, right. Just the weekend?" He leaned up from the counter.

"Yeah, you know Wes ... busy, busy, busy." Quisha brushed her hair from her face as she said this.

"Has he decided what to do for his birthday yet?" At the end of the month, June the thirtieth to be precise, was Wesley's birthday. Finally he had reached the big Three O. Quisha's stool made a sound like fingernails on a blackboard as she got up to put her glass in the sink.

"Well, he said something about checking a place called The Spot in Covent Garden as he knows a friend who plays out there on a Friday night. Says it's guaranteed to be real funky."

Dwayne grinned, "Sounds like my kind of place but I thought Wes would be looking for something more rootsy."

Quisha shrugged.

"Well, I'll probably see him Saturday night, because I'm meeting Kate during the day ... "

Dwayne stopped himself going any further.

"Oh yes?" said Quisha slyly, the tone of her voice egging her brother on.

"It's just casual Quisha ... a chat, then maybe a movie."

Quisha knew when her brother was holding out on her. "A movie eh?" her tone was teasing. "Come on Dwayne, what's happening between you guys ... you know you can tell me."

There was a long pause as Dwayne's brain clicked over. He knew that Quisha meant well and that she had never given him any cause to feel inhibited, but right now he couldn't even identify his own feelings let alone express them. He needed more time.

"Quisha," he began, then rested a hand on her arm, "Sis, right now I don't really know what's happening but let's talk about it later, yeah?" Later meant later, so Quisha knew better than to push him. She switched topic quickly as her brother shifted his weight on the breakfast bench, looking uneasy.

"Hey, did I tell you about the present James bought me yesterday?"

"No, but let me guess ... another bottle of lavender oil?" They both laughed.

Thursday night brought strangers into Dwayne's small box bedroom, into his wet and erotic dreams. His pulse raced as a beautiful black man placed his hands on Dwayne's thighs, rubbing them up and down. Dwayne could hear himself moan as the stranger continued this movement slowly and rhythmically. Dwayne arched his body upward as he pulled the stranger to him. As he did so the face changed from being hard and angular, to being soft and slightly rounded. Breasts now came into view. It was Kate on top of him.

"Take me," she rasped, "take me." He pulled her to him. But then, quite suddenly, from the background, came another familiar face. It was his father.

"Dad?" He could hear the strain in his voice. "Dad what are you doing here?" He looked at his son quietly, disapprovingly.

"You look the same ... " He could pick up the relief in his voice as the words trailed out, "You look the same." The stern face before him was unmoving, disapproval indelibly fixed on his face.

Dwayne woke up in a cold sweat. Years of internalising, assimilating and living by the values of his parents now left Dwayne riddled with guilt. He had not yet learned how to be completely self-sufficient in terms of finding the values, the nourishment that best suited his own growth. Dwayne was beginning to realise that the shackles of convention, guilt, and wretched insecurity could only be broken a bit at a time. He lay rigid now, afraid to close his eyes. He lay there in the dark, waiting for daybreak to come; to lift the weight that pressed so oppressively on both chest and mind. He lay there waiting for the world to become a kinder place.

Friday was spent relatively quietly, with Dwayne writing out a letter of application for the job at Quentin Kineston and posting it with his C.V. to the address in his notebook. There was still no response to his past applications – his thoughts were in limbo.

24

Saturday, Dwayne left the house early, before eight, no-one else was up. As he walked down to Cambridge rail station, he swung his camera absentmindedly by it's strap; to and fro like a great pendulum. He recognised a neighbour coming towards him in the opposite direction. The elderly gentleman was walking his alsation. Dwayne averted his eyes as they came closer to each other. His instinct was now to side-step any potential rejection by taking no risks. Unconsciously he had taken on board the very same strategy that had been so frequently used upon himself and his family. Both parties passed by each other in stilted silence.

When his train pulled into King's Cross, Dwayne alighted and made his way down the Piccadilly Line to Leicester Square. According to his watch it was 9.30a.m., that gave him roughly two hours of photography before he met up with Kate. He loved it around this area. There was a buzz that was vibrant. The streets surrounding the station were varied, as were it's people. You could be anything you wanted here. As he made his way across Soho, crowds, noise and bustle filled his camera lens. The bright morning sun gave the perfect conditions for his 200 A.S.A. camera film. *Clunk* went the heavy shutter time and time again – he was flowing with a creativity he hadn't felt for a long while. Once twenty-four frames had been used up, Dwayne glanced at his watch. 10.36a.m. it read, the gold hands glinting in the sun. He wiped away beads of sweat from his temples with the back of his right hand. Carefully he put the lens cap back on his camera, then slung it over his tired right shoulder. He glanced down the extremely busy Brewer Street that he now found himself on. His bright yellow IRIE vest top clung to his sweaty body. He needed refreshment quickly. The sight of a small girl waving a bright orange ice-lolly in what seemed his direction alerted his mind to the seduction of ice-cream, to be more precise, Haagen Daz. With this in mind he made a bee line for their outlet by the Hippodrome. Thankful of his decision to wear his Reeboks that morning, Dwayne bounced along Wardour Street with an emphasised spring in his step. His mood was carefree as he bounced into the restaurant/café. It had been a good morning and he wanted to treat himself. He glanced at his watch again, it's monologue face alerting him to the fact that he only had forty five minutes in which to eat his ice-cream and then bomb along to the other side of town. He was meeting Kate just out side Hammersmith tube station as that was the closest rendezvous to the Riverside Studio. About to order chocolate fudge, he thought better of it and ordered pecan.

"Will that be a single scoop or a double?" asked the young lady serving.

"Ah, make it a double, please," Dwayne grinned. What the hell, life's too short. He salved his conscience with the thought that at least his resolve to steer clear of chocolate hadn't weakened. Spots were his worst enemy. Meeting up with Kate seemed to deepen his awareness of his own vanity and he smiled inwardly to himself. Loud slurping noises seemed unavoidable as Dwayne hurried towards the tube line, trailing drops of ice-cream on the way.

"Mmm-wa, mm-wa," went Kate's lips as she greeted Dwayne with a continental style kiss on both corners of his mouth.

"Hi," he grinned sheepishly, feeling a little overwhelmed by her enthusiasm and perhaps a little uneasy. Why was Kate always so confident, so sure of herself? There was something unsettling about that, felt Dwayne. It drew further attention to his own inadequacies in that direction. He frowned slightly. Kate oblivious to these thoughts sensed the unease that was in the air, she filled it quickly.

"Five minutes late, tut, tut," her voice was teasing and playful.

"What is this?" snapped Dwayne, feeling somewhat put upon now, "We're not all as efficient and organised as you – we lesser mortals." His words were dry and scathing as he drew away from her. Kate pouted, accentuating the fact that she had scraped her hair back into a pony tail.

"Come on Dwayne, relax, I was only teasing ... come on."

Dwayne felt obliged to do just that, his shoulders dropped and his tone softened.

"Okay, so what time's the film? Did you say one thirty or something?" He could see a slow smirk spread over Kate's face. He noticed now the trendy all-in-one ankle length culottes that she was wearing, the way that the cream cotton flapped about her flat D.M.'s was breezy. He thought it peculiar now to think of her in anything that wasn't either practical or functional. For Kate high heels seemed a total no, no. He wondered if that was part of her attraction or whether ... his thoughts dried up as Kate now took his left hand and proceeded to walk out of the station.

"So that leaves us with time to have a bite of something."

"Uhh ... run that by me again," said Dwayne, realising that he had seen her lips move earlier without hearing the answer to his question.

"I said the movie's on at one, but that at least it still gave us time to have some lunch somewhere, yeah?" Kate was walking briskly now, swinging her hips confidently with an ease and grace that flattered her form. Though not slim, she certainly had a waistline. Though she was not as pretty as some girls, or Candice for that matter, she had a panache that Dwayne couldn't fail to admire. He squeezed her right hand gently as they walked briskly in search of a sandwich bar.

"Any luck with the job hunting?" asked Kate, as they approached Pret A Manger.

"Oh God, don't mention that subject ... still no interviews, not one sausage. I'm fed up with the form-filling and the waiting already. Who knows, maybe I won't even find a teaching job for this year? On the scrap heap before I've even begun." Kate, a little taken aback by this flood of negativity, tried to sound upbeat as she said hesitantly, "A little patience, darling ... a little patience."

As they stood outside of the door to Pret A Manger, Dwayne gazed into Kate's eyes, surprise and bewilderment written all over his face. She said darling. Dwayne felt the last vestige of doubt dissolve as he kissed Kate lightly on the lips.

"Who's paying for lunch then, darling?"

After viewing this particular screening of the compulsive French film, *Betty Blue*, Dwayne couldn't stop ranting about it. Kate on the other hand was somewhat subdued as she wondered about their future together; about how her parents would react to the news of her having a black boyfriend, or was it partner now? She wasn't sure. She wondered about the next few weeks of the summer, the time that she would share with this man that touched her so. She felt excited. Fate had finally shone on her, bringing her the love that she needed so very much.

As Kate stood waving at Dwayne, the train moved from it's moorings on platform 11B, then lurched, gathering pace as it pulled out of King's Cross. She thought about his invitation to the club in Covent Garden.

"A chance to meet his brother and sister," he had said, "to have a good time, to celebrate." They had a lot to celebrate. She touched her lips gently and thought of the long, intimate kiss they had shared just a few minutes ago. The feel of his tongue was still there. The warm spicy scent of his aftershave lingered in her nostrils. She felt less brazen now as she stood on the platform alone. She had never kissed anyone intimately in public before. It was both exhilarating and unnerving at the same time. Kate sighed. She was missing Dwayne already. The end of the month seemed so far away, though in fact it was only a fortnight away. Still, she thought, if money's short and he has to borrow from his mum, it would be selfish of her to expect him to visit her on a regular basis. But then again, what was stopping her from visiting Cambridge? Well, he hadn't invited her for one and anyway, perhaps it was best not to appear too eager. After all it was still early days. Her heart sang to her all the way home.

Making the soporific journey back to Cambridge, Dwayne leaned back in his seat and yawned. It had been a great day. One to be savoured and slotted into the memory banks for retrieval when days went badly. As fields and trees swept by in the evening sky, a picture of Kate's smiling face came into his head. Her eyes aflame with Mediterranean passion. A woman who now shared a place in his heart. It seemed strange to admit to himself that he was in love with this woman, actually in love, at a time when love seemed furthest from his mind, when job hunting and independence had replaced his focus. Life seemed so contradictory at times. It seemed strange to finally have a lover of whatever sex, someone who wanted to be with him and vice versa, someone he wanted to be with. Dwayne's mind danced along as he tried to imagine what sex with Kate would be like. Would it be intense, hot and passionate, or slow and meandering, experimental. His body shuddered slightly; imperceptible to those sitting opposite or to the side of him. He took a cursory glance at them anyway, just to be certain.

To break the sensation of chug, chugging in his stomach, Dwayne decided to make a trip to the toilet cubicle. As usual it was poorly maintained and stank of urine. So much for the customer charter, he thought to himself as he shut the door behind him. The lock made a metallic clunk as it changed from vacant to engaged. Suddenly the train lurched, flinging Dwayne roughly to the far wall of the cubicle, causing him to press the palms of his hands up against the small frosted window instinctively. He cast his eyes upward and saw a small red chain. Beneath it were the words ALARM - £50 FINE FOR IMPROPER USE. It amused him now as he imagined the chaos that would have followed if he had held on to the chain for support, thinking it was there for such a purpose. He felt giddy and happy. His mind was light, bubbly almost, as it searched for further distraction. Taking up a stance as if going into battle with a sumo wrestler, Dwayne unfastened his zip and got on with the business to hand. EEEEEE...! The train entered a tunnel as Dwayne tried clumsily to make his way out of the cubicle back to his seat. EEEEEEEEEEEEEEEEE...

25

It was ten past nine when Dwayne finally put his key into the front door and entered the house. He could hear the drone of the newsreader's voice emanating from the living room. The large black roll bag in the middle of the hallway was a less than subtle reminder that Wesley was home.

"Hi," offered Dwayne meekly in the hushed atmosphere surrounding his family as they sat fixed in the bright illumination of the television screen.

"Hi Dwayne," said his mother keenly, as she turned to face him. Her broad smile warming him on this already warm summer's evening.

"Yo bro," said Wesley, smirking from his position on the settee beside Hyacinth. He gave a high five salute. Quisha, closest to the telly sat in an easy chair.

"Hi," she said in an almost half-whisper, half-turning to face her brother, half-focusing on the television. Dwayne turned to leave.

"One sec, Dwayne." It was Wesley. He hauled himself from the settee and made a gesture to Dwayne that he would follow as he wanted a word. They both made their way up the stairs and into Dwayne's room.

Dwayne sat cross-legged on the top of the bed with his back resting on the headboard, whilst Wesley sat on the edge of the bed, twisting slightly to face his brother. Dwayne smiled wryly as he thought about Kate again – the fact he had a lover would come as a surprise to his brother as up to now they had kept the embargo on each other's love life. Just as quickly the smile turned to a look of despair, a horrible thought grabbed him. Suppose this relationship with Kate was just another illusion like the other times – just as he relaxed into thinking he had found love it would disappear like an apparition. He imagined love as a butterfly; rush in with your net and it takes flight. Was he rushing now? Was he too eager to open his heart once more? He could feel his chest tighten as doubts and fears came back to haunt him. His lungs felt as though they were seizing up as he struggled to take the air down. He sensed that he was panicking, heightening his distress.

"Bro, are you okay?" asked his brother gently, resting his hand on his knee. Dwayne couldn't answer; all of his energies were consumed with fighting the battle inside. 'Relax Dwayne, relax, for God's sake *relax*'. He moved the thought around in his head. His breathing eased. Dwayne saw the screwed features of his brother's worry.

"It's okay," he half-smiled. "I sometimes get a strange feeling in my chest ... just makes it hard to breath. I must be still recovering from the stress of the last year ... you know, the course and everything. Come on, I'm fine, really." Swiftly changing tack, he decided against a full scale exposé of his love life. "So what's happening with you Wes. Come on, fill me in." Wesley looked a little less worried now and his facial expression eased.

"Well ... Quisha told you about the plans I'm making for The Spot, yeah." This was a statement rather than a question. "But I wondered if you're alright for money ... you know, for the train fare up there? Quisha mentioned something about you having cash flow problems ... " His words trailed off. Dwayne sighed.

"Yeah, my student loan's run out," he struggled now to make light of it. "Still, if I ... " he corrected himself, "when I get a job I can start living it up again. Weekend breaks to New York, that kind of thing." They both laughed at this. "If only I was as thrifty as you, eh Wes?" Wesley curtailed his laughter as he was just a tad tired of being labelled thrifty. In his family that amounted to stingy. Though generous with his money Wesley felt that Dwayne was maybe on the reckless side when it came to such matters. Still, he didn't want to get uppity on something said in jest.

"Anyway," said Wesley after a pause, "if you are strapped, Quisha reckons that James might as well drive us all down." Dwayne beamed at this suggestion. Wesley continued. "Only trouble is that James likes his drink when he's out, so he would rather everyone took the train – still Quisha can talk him round." The left-hand corner of Wesley's mouth went up in a wry smile. Dwayne looked glum; the thought of putting James out did not rest easily with him at all.

"Oh, by the way," Dwayne tried to sound as nonchalant as possible, "I've invited a friend along ... her name's Kate ... " Wesley's eyebrows perked up, "we met at Goldsmith's. That's okay with you, isn't it?"

"Oh sure," said Wesley hurriedly, "The more the merrier." His broad features splayed into a knowing grin. The blue of the room's light shone strangely into his wide, open eyes. Dwayne looked down briefly, eyes cast on his fingernails and deep blue bedspread. Sensing the discord that loomed Wesley tactfully went on to other things. "So tell me about the job hunt. How's it going?" Dwayne's look of despondency told all – the conversation seemed to be heading for rocky ground – but Wesley was out of tact and pressed on. "Hey don't look like that, now that you've found yourself a woman, I'm sure the rest will fall into place. Things are working out for you." There was a pause.

"What the hell does finding a partner have to do with a job?" asked Dwayne, somewhat outraged.

"Well," stammered Wesley hesitantly, "at least having sorted out this notion of ... of" he could hardly get the words out, "of bisexuality ... you can now focus on ... well, you know, job prospects and whatever ... " His words dried up as he saw the anger rise to Dwayne's lips.

"Find a woman! Find a woman! That's your answer to everything isn't it? When the hell are you going to grow up Wesley!!? When are you going to realise that not everyone sees life the way you do!?"

This was a statement that left Wesley reeling. He left the room without answering; without acquiescence; and without understanding his brother any more than he had done the fifteen minutes before entering his room. 'Damn, damn, damn'. Dwayne cursed himself repeatedly. He had lost his temper yet again. A new thought entered his mind, 'Hadn't he thought only a few days ago to break this pattern of confrontation to somehow rise above the situation?' He clambered to his feet and rushed out of his room, catching Wesley as he entered his own room across the landing.

"Hey Wes, I'm sorry. I shouldn't have shouted," he rested a hand tentatively on his brother's elbow, "I'm just tired, okay."

Wesley turned, a little surprised by this change in events. He felt suddenly warm towards his brother, and stammered,

"Ahh, okay bro, I can relate to that. Maybe I was jumping the gun a little, eh? ... Being a little thoughtless." They smiled at each other. Another step had been taken.

26

The following day Quisha and Dwayne took a walk along the river Cam, along were it winds itself around the back of the colleges. Dressed in a pair of sling backs and a long African print dress, Quisha looked Nubian. Her dark skin shimmered with cocoa butter, attracting admirers who went unnoticed. Her full concentration was on her brother and what he had to say as they idled along the riverbank arm-in-arm. With Dwayne, Quisha always felt completely held. There was an intensity about Dwayne that she hadn't really identified before today.

"You've been so pensive these last few days Dwayne. It's not like you to keep things bottled up. You know you can always talk to me ... don't you?" Slight hurt was in her voice.

"I know Sis," said Dwayne soothingly, "it's just that ... well there's times when I need to work things out on my own ... you know?" His sister smiled weakly. Dwayne carried on, hazy sunlight reflecting off his shades. "Well, I guess you've realised that Kate's been on my mind a lot lately and ... ah, we've decided to start seeing each other." A light breeze blew Quisha's hair behind her.

"Ha, ha," she laughed in a deliberate manner, "I knew it ... I knew you were serious about her. Jees, that's cool Dwayne, I'm happy for you," she squeezed her arm tightly around his as she spoke the words.

"Thanks Sis," he replied, "but don't let on to Mum yet, okay, I don't want her to get carried away. I just can't take anymore pressure right now." Quisha gave him a knowing glance.

"Thank God for sunny days," she said now taking in the scenery. "Ah, look at the cute little ducklings." She pointed over to the two fawn-coloured birds with black speckles scattered haphazardly on the soft down of their tail feathers. They were moving playfully in circles around what looked like their mother. They watched them for a few minutes before moving on, arms still linked. "Any thoughts about Wesley's present?" asked Quisha after a long silence.

"Mmm ... not yet," answered Dwayne, having given it no thought whatsoever up until then.

"I thought maybe we could all chip in for a gold-plated pen set or something in the jewellery line." Quisha's tone was non-committal.

Dwayne laughed. "Oh yes, a gold medallion maybe. Really cool."

"No, stupid!" chuckled Quisha light-heartedly. "I was thinking of a nice signet ring."

"Ah, I see ... " Dwayne's voice trailed off as they ducked their heads down under the trailing branches of a willow partially blocking the path along which they walked. He carried on as they struggled through the screen of foliage, "Does Mum have any ideas?"

"I'm not sure," replied Quisha, a little hesitantly, her concentration now taken up with trying to extricate a clump of her hair from the branches of the willow, "I haven't ... damn," her hair had snagged again, "I haven't had a chance to bring it up with Mum yet." Having cleared the obstacle both sister and brother continued along the path arm-in-arm.

"Have you had a chance to call James yet about driving us down to London?" Dwayne turned to face Quisha briefly to read her expression as he put forward this question.

"Mmmm ... no not as yet," Quisha's lips scrunched slightly, "but I'm sure it's not a problem," her words rang with certainty. Dwayne wondered if he too would come to know Kate with such clarity, such surety. He almost envied the bond that tied his sister to another man at times. He wondered now why she hadn't pressed him into telling her more about Kate. Whether she was fat or thin; funny or serious. Closed or open. Then again she was not one to press; unlike himself she had incredible patience. They walked on for a while in silence, distracted by their own thoughts. Then quite suddenly Quisha let go of her brother's arm and made an almighty sneeze as pollen was forced out of her nose.

"Woo ... we had better turn back Dwayne, my eyes are getting itchy and I've left my hayfever tablets at home."

"Okay," he nodded casually before doing an about turn on his heels. Quisha sneezed again before doing the same.

"Bloody pollen," she cursed, as she linked arms with her brother once more. "Hey, you lucky bugger," she chided, "I wish I was on holiday right now."

"Ha," snorted Dwayne, "some holiday, I can't even relax. I have to worry about finding myself a job otherwise I'm up the creek without a paddle?"

"Mmm, I guess ... " Quisha was interrupted.

"I mean looking for a job is a full-time job in itself," Dwayne's tone was rasping now.

"I hear you ... I hear you," responded Quisha, knowing only too well that eliciting sympathy for her own predicament would be hopeless at this stage. "Just think," she said changing the direction of conversation, "This time last year we were all in J.A." Her brother smiled. They both walked on, happy to be joined by memories as well as by blood.

At last Wednesday brought with it the promise of an interview at Quentin Kineston in one week's time. Dwayne breathed a sigh of relief as he put the typed letter back into it's manila envelope. He started to say something, then realised that no-one was there. It still seemed strange being at home with everyone else at work. He followed this thought into the kitchen where he made some breakfast – if pouring milk on Weetabix can be called making breakfast. Morning sun flooded the room whilst tiny specks of rain spattered on the window. Dwayne munched on his cereal, glad now for an excuse to visit London, and hopefully his girlfriend, before his brother's birthday. He hated the power that money now exerted over him; hated the fact that he now had to go cap in hand to borrow money from his mother; and hated the fact that due to some strange discomfort he had felt unable to invite his girlfriend up to Cambridge. He pondered over this last point. If he had invited her to Cambridge wouldn't that really mean inviting her to meet his mother. What message would that send out? Wasn't it too early in their relationship for such a meeting? What if she came to Cambridge without coming to the house – would his mum feel hurt if she found out? Things were complicated enough between them already. He rose from the breakfast bench, moving with his bowl over to the sink, sure in his mind that things were best left as they were. He dunked his cereal bowl into the sudsy washing-up water.

That night Dwayne called Kate to let her know the good news; that they could meet each other after the interview; that he cared about her and loved her, and that he felt blessed to have her in his life. That same night he caressed her, licked her, made love to her, but only in his dreams.

27

The next couple of days were largely uneventful. They were basically spent with Dwayne sleeping, eating, and enjoying the novelty of having nothing planned. It was simply a time to relax and to charge the batteries. Batteries that had been running on nervous energy for some time.

Saturday morning was absolutely gorgeous, the hottest day all summer and not a cloud in the sky. Hyacinth, Quisha, and Dwayne had all been up for several hours now. They were all spread-eagled on top of sheets spread over the garden lawn. They were doing what, to all intense and purposes, has been deemed suicidal in our present climate of ozone depletion. Yes, they were sunbathing, roasting themselves slowly until their skins turned the beautiful even colour that nature had predetermined, quite in contrast to the blotchy paleness of winter.

A wonderful scene of vibrance, energy, and colour filled the garden. Hyacinth's favourite corner of the garden was a mass of yellows, pinks, purples, and scarlets. What was left uncovered of the garden was lush and green with only the odd daisy breaking up the colour. Shocking red flowers showed their friendly faces as they poked through the wooden slatted fence which divided their garden from the neighbour's immediately to the left of them. Ironically the flowers were far more eager to make their acquaintance than the owners. It was Jamaica that Dwayne now thought of as he lay back and drew in the sunlight. Jamaica and the sun-drenched beach of Hellshire. Next to him Hyacinth's face glowed with lashings of sweet-smelling cocoa butter. Dwayne's thoughts switched to the strange smell that now hung in the air as cocoa butter mingled with Quisha's infusion of sandalwood oil from the Body Shop, not to mention the roses, daisies and ... his thoughts were interrupted.

"Are you nervous about Wednesday, Dwayne?" Hyacinth turned her face on it's side in order to face her son.

"Mmm ... oh, the interview. Yeah I guess, but I'm trying not to think about it really ... so as I don't, you know get anxious and scr... - well, mess up." Hyacinth smiled.

"You won't mess up son ... not as long as you're ... well, yourself." Dwayne shifted his position slightly so that the sun wasn't in his eyes. This was the most supportive thing his mum had said to him in a long while. He touched her hand briefly.

"Thanks Mum." He didn't know what else to say. He looked over at Quisha, she smiled.

"We're rooting for you," she said, squinting into the sunlight, her hair shining unnaturally with oil. There was a look of compassion even though her eyes were scrunched.

"Thanks Sis." Dwayne touched her on the side of the face, then said, "Hey, I'm afraid that I'll have to ask you for another loan though Mum ... forty pounds or so ... can you manage that?"

"Sure," she said without looking at him this time. After a brief pause she asked, "How do you both feel about getting Wesley a travel bag for his birthday as he's always on the go ... a real wanderer that boy. I saw a beautiful black leather one in Robert Sayles last week."

"That sounds great," enthused Quisha.

"Yeah, I like it too," added Dwayne quickly. "Nice one, Mum."

Hyacinth smiled briefly with satisfaction, then turned over for the sun to bake her back.

"Hey, I spoke to James, Dwayne, and driving us up to London is cool with him, okay?"

"Ah, right ... good old James." He mopped his forehead with his right hand, "I'm going to catch a quick swim before lunch," said Dwayne, as he struggled to his feet. "It's too hot to be sunning myself all day ... I need to cool off," he chuckled lightly.

"Where are you going, Parkside?" enquired Quisha.

"Yeah, why do you want to come?" Dwayne slipped his perforated vest top back on.

"Mmm ... naa thanks, Dwayne," she sniggered in a cosy manner, "I'll just laze here with Mum a while longer. But have a good time yeah?"

"Sure," said Dwayne over his shoulder. Knowing that his mum hated chlorine he didn't bother to extend the invitation to her. "See you later!" he shouted as he re-entered the house to pick up the necessaries.

"Bye!" came the dual response.

Rank chlorine vapour hung in the air immediately outside the swimming baths. It was one of those anomalies that once one entered the building the gas no longer seemed so pungent. Dwayne slipped his money through the glass window and thanked the cashier for his token. On entering the crowded changing room he could hear yelps and screams emanating from the pool itself. He jostled past an overweight man of forty-something with a flabby stomach. He noticed how varied and interesting were the body shapes that now surrounded him. He wondered about the stories that they themselves told. The experiences that had gone into shaping them and indeed the minds that connected them to those very experiences. As Dwayne undressed he felt a little self-conscious. It had been a while since he had stripped in public and somehow breaking patterns always seemed to involve some level of discomfort. After grappling with his swimming trunks for a couple of minutes, he became aware of a presence to his left. The sort of presence created when someone is staring at you with an intensity that alerts even those senses usually left dormant. Dwayne looked to his left along the bench as he pulled the trunks securely around his waist. There stood one of the most attractive men he had ever come across. He stood there deliberately meeting Dwayne's eyes; willing his attention. His eyes were immediately dark and seductive, his features slim and refined, his skin a yellow-brown. He stood with his towel in hand, dripping from his shower. Dwayne's impulse was to smile. The stranger did the same.

"Cold in there," he remarked in a friendly tone as he wiped moisture from his bulky but defined frame.

"Oh, is it?" Dwayne felt a little awkward.

"Still," continued the stranger, "just what you need on a hot day like this."

"Yeah," Dwayne answered back.

"Probably why it's so crowded today," continued the stranger leisurely whilst rubbing his short black hair. Dwayne noticed the slight bend in each lock that gave away his mixed parentage. "Hey," said the stranger, moving in closer, "my name's Gary." He offered his right hand whilst clinging to his towel in the left. Dwayne tried to keep his eyes above waist level. But Gary's carefree openness begged a certain brash but modest admiration.

"Ah," stumbled Dwayne, "my name's Dwayne." He shook the stranger's hand firmly whilst glancing quickly into his eyes. A knowing smile crept over Gary's face.

"Maybe I'll catch you later ... upstairs in the coffee bar?"

"Yeah ... maybe," answered Dwayne, a little unsure of himself. Just before moving off Dwayne gave a smile at the clean-shaven face that attracted him so. Gary smiled back whilst drying his ample crotch with the white cotton towel.

As the cool water buoyed Dwayne's body, he paced up and down, steadily stretching his torso into the breast stroke. Inside a storm raged. Why the hell did life have to be so unpredictable? He couldn't believe this twist of fate. It took time to digest. Here he was, finally in a loving relationship after waiting so long , and then life pulls this on him. Challenges his sense of security and self. Kate up to now hadn't mentioned any concerns, if she had any, about infidelity. Was she so trusting in him and in herself that the question never arose? Perhaps there was a tacit understanding between them. Or was it a question of timing? By the same token he hadn't brought the topic up, it had never occurred to him until now. After all hadn't society told him that he was the partner more likely to feel constrained by monogamy. He was a man and a bisexual man at that. The thoughts thundered around in his head. Maybe the most pertinent question right now was did Gary even fancy him? Of course, he did – they both knew he did. He realised that it was crunch time. It was time he found an answer to the one question he never imagined having to confront ... did he want monogamy in a relationship? Was he prepared to make a choice? Dwayne's thoughts were becoming incoherent as he begun to thrash in the water, exhausted from thought. He gasped for air as someone's feet pushed water into his face. He pushed on as chlorine filled his lungs. He was choking and spluttering now but at least he could wade as he had made it to the shallow end.

"Hi," said Gary calmly as Dwayne approached his seat, hair still damp.

"Hi," replied Dwayne sweetly.

Gary continued, "I was watching you through the window here ... have a look." Dwayne peered through the window immediately to the side of the table. It gave a clear view of the pool below them. "I like your style," Gary's gravely tone gave no indication of what he meant by this. Was he talking about his general appearance or staccato technique in the water? Dwayne guessed at it being the former. He smiled at this point, not quite sure how to respond; a gentle smile that was both warm and open. He then looked out over the pool. Both were silent. Dwayne thought about the word 'style' and glanced again in Gary's direction but only briefly. His eyes were refreshed with the memory of Gary's crisp khaki-coloured jeans; tight ribbed, white T-shirt with 'LOVE IT' stencilled across the chest. The chunky stainless steel wrist watch had a sporty look about it and itself said something about it's owner. When it came to style Gary spoke volumes and to Dwayne's thinking that meant he was on his side of the FM dial. "So what do you do?" Gary's voice broke the silence.

"Oh, well, I'm in the teaching profession, but I've only just finished the training."

Gary's eyes lit up with glee. "Hey that's cool." His voice went a little high with interest. "I'm in education also... as a lab technician at the Long Road Sixth Form College."

"Oh, right," Dwayne smiled, "Do you enjoy what you do?"

"Sure," answered Gary, "It's kind of relaxed." Conversation drifted on between them as they picked out the threads of their past and wove them together in the present. It was clear to Dwayne as he finally parted company with Gary that he had made a friend that day. But what kind of friend? Gary's intense questions surrounding his relationship with Kate and subsequent allusions to sexual experimentation with and without women left no doubt in his mind that this man was quite happy to explore the realms of three in a bed. The term free spirit certainly seemed to crop up quite often during the conversation as Dwayne recollected. As Dwayne walked towards home he wondered if he too was a free spirit – was Kate? As he crossed the junction leading into his street he thought of how much he loved Kate, needed her. As he turned the door key in the lock he thought of the lingering impression that Gary's warm hand had left in his. And as he slammed the door shut he resolved in his mind to have Gary in his life, but only as a friend, it was safer.

28

"Come in please," said Mrs Green, the Head of Art at Quentin Kineston secondary school. She shook Dwayne's hand cordially as she showed him into the Principal's office. Behind a long narrow wooden desk sat a lady of middle years and a slightly younger man. The man, who was clearly balding, had a look of rigour in his stern features and starched grey suit. He introduced himself as Mr Smithe, Vice Principal. This left Ms Henderson, the Principal, to introduce herself last. With a firm grip she said,

"Please sit down." Her long, steel-grey hair was pulled back into an elaborate bun, her cool blue eyes displayed a look of complete control. As she herself sat, Dwayne couldn't help but notice the way her dark navy suit hugged what was evidently a well-honed body. The fitted jacket clasped just so, whilst the conservative skirt attempted to cover taut calf muscles. Images of her in a leather bodice and boots came into Dwayne's head. He couldn't help it. She was now striking the top of the desk with a small black whip. "Do as I say, now sit," she commanded, "I'm your dominatrix ... " Her jaw pulled taut. "What do you have to offer us?" she asked in a hard rasping voice. Dwayne sat up to attention as she struck the desk top once more, her colleagues looked on with glee.

"Umm ... ah ... well." Dwayne was struggling to get the words out, his head filled with confusion and madness.

"I'm going to have to hurry you," she continued impatiently, stroking the end of the whip.

"Well, I'm efficient, conscientious ... " Dwayne stopped in mid-flow as she leaned over her desk toward him, bearing her breasts over the brim of her bodice.

"Pardon," she said indignantly, "You're rather a disobedient young man, aren't you?"

"What?" asked Dwayne, out of more confusion but now also out of nervousness. He couldn't imagine what he had said wrong. His lips quivered.

"Call me mistress when you speak to me – slave!" she slapped him hard across the right cheek and he flinched. But in that flinch was a rush of excitement, a feeling of the taboo. A feeling of wanting someone else to take the reigns, to take control, to take responsibility for his pain. Slap went her hand once more across his face as she glared at him now from her position on top of the desk. "Say it!" she cried, "call me your mistress!"

"Ah ... ah," Dwayne floundered, his words could or would not come out.

"There's a thin line between pain and pleasure," she continued coolly, "which do you want?" Her colleagues were salivating as they awaited his response, almost willing him to give that which he had no desire to give. What should he say? What did he want? What did anyone really want? He opened his mouth as Ms Henderson's painted nails reached once more for obedience, for control. Was it really control of himself that she was after or control of herself, of her life? "Well I'm glad to say that we can offer you the job immediately." Ms Henderson shook his hand firmly and shook her head approvingly. Dwayne was dazed, his mind couldn't take things in ... he couldn't even imagine what had been said. He only knew that he was back in the real world now, with a real job, and that job meant for him a real start. Quite what sort of start was unclear but for Dwayne that didn't matter. He only knew that somewhere up there someone was looking after him. It was a strange but wonderful feeling. He had dared to wish and his wish had been answered.

"Mmmm ... have you missed me darling?" Kate pulled her lips from the wetness of her lover. "I've missed you," she continued without waiting for the reply, but hugging him closely.

"I've missed you too," he whispered into her ear. They were at the entrance of Notting Hill Gate tube station where they had agreed to meet for dinner. "I've got it," he murmured, "I've got the job." He drew back his head and smiled into his girlfriend's eyes.

"Oh ... that's brilliant Dwayne, I knew you'd get it ... I just knew it!" she hugged him again. He returned her hug with his own delicate warmth and vulnerability. Letting out a long quiet sigh, he felt how good it was to be in love and to have love in one's life. They walked hand in hand along the main road, oblivious to traffic, people, and noise; lost in each other's loving aura. Dwayne had meant to tell Kate about Gary, but didn't.

Saturday had arrived and that meant party night.

"Hi James," said Hyacinth sweetly as she opened the door for her daughter's boyfriend.

"Hi," he said casually, totally dismissive of past pretensions and formality.

"God knows why Quisha and Dwayne aren't ready yet?" she continued in a chatty manner, ushering him into the living room, as she shrieked, "Quisha! Dwayne! James is here now." She smiled somewhat apologetically into his kind, smooth face. He ruffled his thick straight hair a little, then said,

"Shame you couldn't come really."

Hyacinth chuckled lightly, "Heh, that's a young person's place," she smiled for a moment at some distant thought, then said, "You're looking smart by the way, is the shirt new?" James looked down at his silk Armani shirt and laughed.

"A little treat for myself, you know." Hyacinth smiled once more. Before anything else could be said, Quisha and Dwayne came thudding down the stairs, both in the bare minimum for modesty and both ready for action.

Dwayne was apprehensive now as they drew up to the club, having picked up Kate on the way. He had gone over this moment again and again in his mind, when he would finally introduce her to his brother. With Quisha there was no real apprehension as she had always showed such a trust in him. He wondered how Wesley would feel about Kate. Would he like her, warm to her; accept her the way he had, love her for the loving person that she was? Somehow, though not an extension of him, Kate had qualities that mirrored him. Thus how his family reacted to her was as much a statement about him as about her. Though no longer needing approval from them he did desire harmony between his relationships.

Quisha was already talking to Kate from her vantage point in the front passenger seat like a long lost sister and now all that remained was for Wesley to meet her. His heart fluttered as she squeezed his hand, approaching the entrance of The Spot, from which funky rare grooves were instantly audible. Wesley grinned a wide ecstatic grin from just inside the doorway. Although he hadn't mentioned bringing anyone along, a slim elegant woman stood beside him, clasping his left arm a little nervously.

"Hi, you guys made it." Wesley hugged Quisha as she kissed him on the cheek,
"Mm-wa, happy birthday, Wes." Dwayne patted his brother warmly on the shoulder,
"Happy birthday from me too." Dwayne quickly turned to Kate.
"Wesley this is Kate, Kate ... Wesley." His brother stretched out a hand to take hers.
"Nice to meet you," he said cordially, whilst looking at his brother as if to say, you dark horse.
"Same here," offered Kate warmly.
"Happy birthday Wesley," piped up James, who was already beginning to feel a little left out. Dwayne looked at James apologetically as he realised that perhaps he had been a little over eager in the initial introductions. In effect squeezing out poor old James, a soon-to-be family member. He groaned to himself inwardly, what a gaff. Quisha held on to James's hand once more as everyone walked inside where the music was kicking.

Dwayne felt woozy and heady as he slammed the car door shut and snuggled up to Kate in the back seat. "Did you have a good time darling?" he cooed into her ear. Her eyes looked dreamy and tender; not from tiredness but from love. Three o'clock in the morning meant nothing right now. She kissed her boyfriend gently on the lips before answering.
"It was great," she purred. "One of the best nights of my life." Her face was flushed. Dwayne leaned back and yawned, as the car lurched into the quiet road that would take them all home.
EEEEEEEEEEEE...! Rubber screamed against tarmac. WHAM!! Quisha, James, Kate, and Dwayne were thrown forward as the car collided with a stationary Volvo saloon. Dwayne's head crunched against the back of Quisha's seat and then everything went dark as his eyelids closed. He couldn't comprehend what had happened. They had been laughing and joking only seconds before. They had all shared a joke that James had told. That was all he could remember now, as he sat there unable to move. Unable to register whether he was dead or alive; in pain or insane. He was simply there: numb – in limbo. Again the question: was he dead? No answer. His life was not flashing in a haze before him; there were no bright lights. Just a nothingness – a stillness – a gap.

After a period of this nothingness, Dwayne recognised the sound of a voice. "Dwayne, Dwayne, Dwayne," it grew louder, "Dwayne, *Dwayne*! Say something ... for God's sake, say something!" It was a voice that Dwayne recognised but couldn't distinguish. He tried to open his eyes, but nothing. "DWAYNE!!" The voice grew desperate. He could see his family now, one by one, he was kissing them. He could see Kate now and he could see himself kissing her tenderly on the lips. Then he saw Gary and kissed him also on the lips. Finally he saw his dad and for the first time since his death, Dwayne felt calm, peaceful, loving recognition. In his heart he had forgiven his father for the pain he had caused him, for the lack of understanding, for the bigotry and disapproval sown in the oh so distant past. The past that had laid down the cast iron morals that were to shackle his son for so many years to come. Shackles from which he had been unable to break completely free. Dwayne felt tears flowing freely down his cheeks as the last vestiges of pain seeped from his body. It now occurred to him that he was alive – he was still alive – perhaps by the grace of God. His eyes opened wide, inviting the next chapter of his life to begin.